lullaby

Also by Chuck Palahniuk

Fight Club

Survivor

Invisible Monsters

Choke

Doubleday

New York London Toronto

Sydney Auckland

Your Bones, but Words Will Never Hurt You

lullaby

a novel

Chuck Palahniuk

PUBLISHED BY DOUBLEDAY
a division of Random House, Inc.
1540 Broadway, New York, New York 10036

DOUBLEDAY and the portrayal of an anchor with a dolphin are trademarks of
Doubleday, a division of Random House, Inc.

Book design by Dana Leigh Treglia

Library of Congress Cataloging-in-Publication Data

Palahniuk, Chuck.
   Lullaby : a novel / Chuck Palahniuk.— 1st ed.
      p. cm.
    1. Sudden infant death syndrome—Fiction.   2. Incantations—Fiction.
   3. Journalists—Fiction.   I. Title.
   PS3566.A4554 L86 2002

                      2001052979

ISBN 0-385-50447-0
Copyright © 2002 by Chuck Palahniuk

PRINTED IN THE UNITED STATES OF AMERICA

October 2002
First Edition

10 9 8 7 6 5

lullaby

Prologue

At first, the new owner pretends he never looked at the living room floor. Never really looked. Not the first time they toured the house. Not when the inspector showed them through it. They'd measured rooms and told the movers where to set the couch and piano, hauled in everything they owned, and never really stopped to look at the living room floor. They pretend.

Then on the first morning they come downstairs, there it is, scratched in the white-oak floor:

GET OUT

Some new owners pretend a friend has done it as a joke. Others are sure it's because they didn't tip the movers.

A couple of nights later, a baby starts to cry from inside the north wall of the master bedroom.

This is when they usually call.

And this new owner on the phone is not what our hero, Helen Hoover Boyle, needs this morning.

This stammering and whining.

What she needs is a new cup of coffee and a seven-letter word for "poultry." She needs to hear what's happening on the police scanner. Helen Boyle snaps her fingers until her secretary looks in from the outer office. Our hero wraps both hands around the mouthpiece and points the telephone receiver at the scanner, saying, "It's a code nine-eleven."

And her secretary, Mona, shrugs and says, "So?"

So she needs to look it up in the codebook.

And Mona says, "Relax. It's a shoplifter."

Murders, suicides, serial killers, accidental overdoses, you can't wait until this stuff is on the front page of the newspaper. You can't let another agent beat you to the next rainmaker.

Helen needs the new owner at 325 Crestwood Terrace to shut up a minute.

Of course, the message appeared in the living room floor. What's odd is the baby doesn't usually start until the third night. First the phantom message, then the baby cries all night. If the owners last long enough, they'll be calling in another week about the face that appears, reflected in the water when you fill the bathtub. A wadded-up face of wrinkles, the eyes hollowed-out dark holes.

The third week brings the phantom shadows that circle around and around the dining room walls when everybody is seated at the table. There might be more events after that, but nobody's lasted a fourth week.

To the new owner, Helen Hoover Boyle says, "Unless you're ready to go to court and prove the house is unlivable, unless you can prove beyond a shadow of a doubt that the previous owners knew this was happening . . ." She says, "I have to tell you." She says, "You lose a case like this, after you generate all this bad publicity, and that house will be worthless."

It's not a bad house, 325 Crestwood Terrace, English Tudor, newer composition roof, four bedrooms, three and a half baths. An in-ground pool. Our hero doesn't even have to look at the fact sheet. She's sold this house six times in the past two years.

Another house, the New England saltbox on Eton Court, six bedrooms, four baths, pine-paneled entryway, and blood running down the kitchen walls, she's sold that house eight times in the past four years.

To the new owner, she says, "Got to put you on hold for a minute," and she hits the red button.

Helen, she's wearing a white suit and shoes, but not snow white. It's more the white of downhill skiing in Banff with a private car and driver on call, fourteen pieces of matched luggage, and a suite at the Hotel Lake Louise.

To the doorway, our hero says, "Mona? Moonbeam?" Louder, she says, "Spirit-Girl?"

She drums her pen against the folded newspaper page on her desk and says, "What's a three-letter word for 'rodent'?"

The police scanner gargles words, mumbles and barks, repeating "Copy?" after every line. Repeating "Copy?"

Helen Boyle shouts, "This coffee is not going to cut it."

In another hour, she needs to be showing a Queen Anne, five bedrooms, with a mother-in-law apartment, two gas fireplaces, and the face of a barbiturate suicide that appears late at night in the powder room mirror. After that, there's a split-level ranch with FAG heat, a sunken conversation pit, and the reoccurring phantom gunshots of a double homicide that happened over a decade ago. This is all in her thick daily planner, thick and bound in what looks like red leather. This is her record of everything.

She takes another sip of coffee and says, "What do you call this? Swiss Army mocha? Coffee is supposed to taste like coffee."

Mona comes to the doorway with her arms folded across her front and says, "What?"

And Helen says, "I need you to swing by"—she shuffles some

fact sheets on her blotter—"swing by 4673 Willmont Place. It's a Dutch Colonial with a sunroom, four bedrooms, two baths, and an aggravated homicide."

The police scanner says, "Copy?"

"Just do the usual," Helen says, and she writes the address on a note card and holds it out. "Don't resolve anything. Don't burn any sage. Don't exorcise shit."

Mona takes the note card and says, "Just check it for vibes?"

Helen slashes the air with her hand and says, "I don't want anybody going down any tunnels toward any bright light. I want these freaks staying right here, on this astral plane, thank you." She looks at her newspaper and says, "They have all eternity to be dead. They can hang around in that house another fifty years and rattle some chains."

Helen Hoover Boyle looks at the blinking hold light and says, "What did you pick up at the six-bedroom Spanish yesterday?"

And Mona rolls her eyes at the ceiling. She pushes out her jaw and blows a big sigh, straight up to flop the hair on her forehead, and says, "There's a definite energy there. A subtle presence. But the floor plan is wonderful." A black silk cord loops around her neck and disappears into the corner of her mouth.

And our hero says, "Screw the floor plan."

Forget those dream houses you only sell once every fifty years. Forget those happy homes. And screw subtle: cold spots, strange vapors, irritable pets. What she needed was blood running down the walls. She needed ice-cold invisible hands that pull children out of bed at night. She needed blazing red eyes in the dark at the foot of the basement stairs. That and decent curb appeal.

The bungalow at 521 Elm Street, it has four bedrooms, original hardware, and screams in the attic.

The French Normandy at 7645 Weston Heights has arched windows, a butler's pantry, leaded-glass pocket doors, and a body that appears in the upstairs hallway with multiple stab wounds.

The ranch-style at 248 Levee Place—five bedrooms, four and a

4

half baths with a brick patio—it has the reappearing blood coughed up on the master bathroom walls after a drain cleaner poisoning.

Distressed houses, Realtors call them. These houses that never sold because no one liked to show them. No Realtor wanted to host an open house there, risk spending any time there alone. Or these were the houses that sold and sold again every six months because no one could live there. A good string of these houses, twenty or thirty exclusives, and Helen could turn off the police scanner. She could quit searching the obituaries and the crime pages for suicides and homicides. She could stop sending Mona out to check on every possible lead. She could just kick back and find a five-letter word for "equine."

"Plus I need you to pick up my cleaning," she says. "And get some decent coffee." She points her pen at Mona and says, "And out of respect for professionalism, leave the little Rasta doohickeys at home."

Mona pulls the black silk cord until a quartz crystal pops out of her mouth, shining and wet. She blows on it, saying, "It's a crystal. My boyfriend, Oyster, gave it to me."

And Helen says, "You're dating a boy named Oyster?"

And Mona drops the crystal so it hangs against her chest and says, "He says it's for my own protection." The crystal soaks a darker wet spot on her orange blouse.

"Oh, and before you go," Helen says, "get me Bill or Emily Burrows on the phone."

Helen presses the hold button and says, "Sorry about that." She says there are a couple of clear options here. The new owner can move, just sign a quitclaim deed and the house becomes the bank's problem.

"Or," our hero says, "you give me a confidential exclusive to sell the house. What we call a vest-pocket listing."

And maybe the new owner says no this time. But after that hideous face appears between his legs in the bathwater, after the shadows start marching around the walls, well, everyone says yes eventually.

On the phone, the new owner says, "And you won't tell any buyers about the problem?"

And Helen says, "Don't even finish unpacking. We'll just tell people you're in the process of moving out."

If anybody asks, tell them you're being transferred out of town. Tell them you loved this house.

She says, "Everything else will just be our little secret."

From the outer office, Mona says, "I have Bill Burrows on line two."

And the police scanner says, "Copy?"

Our hero hits the next button and says, "Bill!"

She mouths the word *Coffee* at Mona. She jerks her head toward the window and mouths, *Go.*

The scanner says, "Do you copy?"

This *was* Helen Hoover Boyle. Our hero. Now dead but not dead. Here was just another day in her life. This was the life she lived before I came along. Maybe this is a love story, maybe not. It depends on how much I can believe myself.

This is about Helen Hoover Boyle. Her haunting me. The way a song stays in your head. The way you think life should be. How anything holds your attention. How your past goes with you into every day of your future.

That is. This is. It's all of it, Helen Hoover Boyle.

We're all of us haunted and haunting.

On this, the last ordinary day of her regular life, our hero says into the phone, "Bill Burrows?"

She says, "You need to get Emily on the extension because I've just found you two the perfect new home."

She writes the word "horse" and says, "It's my understanding that the sellers are very motivated."

Chapter 1

*T*he problem with every story is you tell it after the fact.

Even play-by-play description on the radio, the home runs and strikeouts, even that's delayed a few minutes. Even live television is postponed a couple seconds.

Even sound and light can only go so fast.

Another problem is the teller. The who, what, where, when, and why of the reporter. The media bias. How the messenger shapes the facts. What journalists call The Gatekeeper. How the presentation is everything.

The story behind the story.

Where I'm telling this from is one café after another. Where I'm writing this book, chapter by chapter, is never the same small town or city or truck stop in the middle of nowhere.

What these places all have in common are miracles. You read

about this stuff in the pulp tabloids, the kind of healings and sightings, the miracles, that never get reported in the mainstream press.

This week, it's the Holy Virgin of Welburn, New Mexico. She came flying down Main Street last week. Her long red and black dreadlocks whipping behind her, her bare feet dirty, she wore an Indian cotton skirt printed in two shades of brown and a denim halter top. It's all in this week's World Miracles Report, next to the cashier in every supermarket in America.

And here I am, a week late. Always one step behind. After the fact.

The Flying Virgin had fingernails painted bright pink with white tips. A French manicure, some witnesses call it. The Flying Virgin used a can of Bug-Off brand insect fogger, and across the blue New Mexican sky, she wrote:

STOP HAVING BABYS

(Sic)

The can of Bug-Off, she dropped. It's right now headed for the Vatican. For analysis. Right now, you can buy postcards of the event. Videos even.

Almost everything you can buy is after the fact. Caught. Dead. Cooked.

In the souvenir videos, the Flying Virgin shakes the can of fogger. Floating above one end of Main Street, she waves at the crowd. And there's a bush of brown hair under her arm. The moment before she starts writing, a gust of wind lifts her skirt, and the Flying Virgin's not wearing any panties. Between her legs, she's shaved.

This is where I'm writing this story from today. Here in a roadside diner, talking to witnesses in Welburn, New Mexico. Here with me is Sarge, a baked potato of an old Irish cop. On the table between us is the local newspaper, folded to show a three-column ad that says:

Attention Patrons of All Plush Interiors
Furniture Stores

The ad says, "If poisonous spiders have hatched from your new upholstered furniture, you may be eligible to take part in a class-action lawsuit." And the ad gives a phone number you could call, but it's no use.

The Sarge has the kind of loose neck skin that if you pinch it, when you let go the skin stays pinched. He has to go find a mirror and rub the skin to make it go flat.

Outside the diner, people are still driving into town. People kneel and pray for another visitation. The Sarge puts his big mitts together and pretends to pray, his eyes rolled sideways to look out the window, his holster unsnapped, his pistol loaded and ready for skeet shooting.

After she was done skywriting, the Flying Virgin blew kisses to people. She flashed a two-finger peace sign. She hovered just above the trees, clutching her skirt closed with one fist, and she shook her red and black dreadlocks back and waved, and Amen. She was gone, behind the mountains, over the horizon. Gone.

Still, you can't trust everything you read in the newspaper.

The Flying Madonna, it wasn't a miracle.

It was magic.

These aren't saints. They're spells.

The Sarge and me, we're not here to witness anything. We're witch-hunters.

Still, this isn't a story about here and now. Me, the Sarge, the Flying Virgin. Helen Hoover Boyle. What I'm writing is the story of how we met. How we got here.

Chapter 2

They ask you just one question. Just before you graduate from journalism school, they tell you to imagine you're a reporter. Imagine you work at a daily big-city newspaper, and one Christmas Eve, your editor sends you out to investigate a death.

The police and paramedics are there. The neighbors, wearing bathrobes and slippers, crowd the hallway of the slummy tenement. Inside the apartment, a young couple is sobbing beside their Christmas tree. Their baby has choked to death on an ornament. You get what you need, the baby's name and age and all, and you get back to the newspaper around midnight and write the story on press deadline.

You submit it to your editor and he rejects it because you don't say the color of the ornament. Was it red or green? You couldn't look, and you didn't think to ask.

With the pressroom screaming for the front page, your choices are: Call the parents and ask the color.

Or refuse to call and lose your job.

This was the fourth estate. Journalism. And where I went to school, just this one question is the entire final exam for the Ethics course. It's an either/or question. My answer was to call the paramedics. Items like this have to be catalogued. The ornament had to be bagged and photographed in some file of evidence. No way would I call the parents after midnight on Christmas Eve.

The school gave my ethics a D.

Instead of ethics, I learned only to tell people what they want to hear. I learned to write everything down. And I learned editors can be real assholes.

Since then, I still wonder what that test was really about. I'm a reporter now, on a big-city daily, and I don't have to imagine anything.

My first real baby was on a Monday morning in September. There was no Christmas ornament. No neighbors crowded around the trailer house in the suburbs. One paramedic sat with the parents in the kitchenette and asked them the standard questions. The second paramedic took me back to the nursery and showed me what they usually find in the crib.

The standard questions paramedics ask include: Who found the child dead? When was the child found? Was the child moved? When was the child last seen alive? Was the child breast- or bottle-fed? The questions seem random, but all doctors can do is gather statistics and hope someday a pattern will emerge.

The nursery was yellow with blue, flowered curtains at the windows and a white wicker chest of drawers next to the crib. There was a white-painted rocking chair. Above the crib was a mobile of yellow plastic butterflies. On the wicker chest was a book open to page 27. On the floor was a blue braided-rag rug. On one wall was a framed needlepoint. It said: *Thursday's Child Has Far to Go*. The room smelled like baby powder.

And maybe I didn't learn ethics, but I learned to pay attention. No detail is too minor to note.

The open book was called *Poems and Rhymes from Around the World*, and it was checked out from the county library.

My editor's plan was to do a five-part series on sudden infant death syndrome. Every year seven thousand babies die without any apparent cause. Two out of every thousand babies will just go to sleep and never wake up. My editor, Duncan, he kept calling it crib death.

The details about Duncan are he's pocked with acne scars and his scalp is brown along the hairline every two weeks when he dyes his gray roots. His computer password is "password."

All we know about sudden infant death is there is no pattern. Most babies die alone between midnight and morning, but a baby will also die while sleeping beside its parents. It can die in a car seat or in a stroller. A baby can die in its mother's arms.

There are so many people with infants, my editor said. It's the type of story that every parent and grandparent is too afraid to read and too afraid not to read. There's really no new information, but the idea was to profile five families that had lost a child. Show how people cope. How people move forward with their lives. Here and there, we could salt in the standard facts about crib death. We could show the deep inner well of strength and compassion each of these people discovers. That angle. Because it ties to no specific event, it's what you'd call soft news. We'd run it on the front of the Lifestyles section.

For art, we could show smiling pictures of healthy babies that were now dead.

We'd show how this could happen to anyone.

That was his pitch. It's the kind of investigative piece you do for awards. It was late summer and the news was slow. This was the peak time of year for last-term pregnancies and newborns.

It was my editor's idea for me to tag along with paramedics.

The Christmas story, the sobbing couple, the ornament, by now I'd been working so long I'd forgotten all that junk.

That hypothetical ethics question, they have to ask that at the end of the journalism program because by then it's too late. You have big student loans to pay off. Years and years later, I think what they're really asking is: *Is this something you want to do for a living?*

Chapter 3

The muffled thunder of dialogue comes through the walls, then a chorus of laughter. Then more thunder. Most of the laugh tracks on television were recorded in the early 1950s. These days, most of the people you hear laughing are dead.

The stomp and stomp and stomp of a drum comes down through the ceiling. The rhythm changes. Maybe the beat crowds together, faster, or it spreads out, slower, but it doesn't stop.

Up through the floor, someone's barking the words to a song. These people who need their television or stereo or radio playing all the time. These people so scared of silence. These are my neighbors. These sound-oholics. These quiet-ophobics.

Laughter of the dead comes through every wall.

These days, this is what passes for home sweet home.

This siege of noise.

After work, I made one stop. The man standing behind the cash register looked up when I limped into the store. Still looking at me, he reached under the counter and brought out something in brown paper, saying, "Double-bagged. I think you'll like this one." He set it on the counter and patted it with one hand.

The package is half the size of a shoe box. It weighs less than a can of tuna.

He pressed one, two, three buttons on the register, and the price window said a hundred and forty-nine dollars. He told me, "Just so you won't worry, I taped the bags shut tight."

In case it rains, he put the package in a plastic bag, and said, "You let me know if there's any of it not there." He said, "You don't walk like that foot is getting better."

All the way home, the package rattled. Under my arm, the brown paper slid and wrinkled. With my every limp, what's inside clattered from one end of the box to the other.

At my apartment, the ceiling is pounding with some fast music. The walls are murmuring with panicked voices. Either an ancient cursed Egyptian mummy has come back to life and is trying to kill the people next door, or they're watching a movie.

Under the floor, there's someone shouting, a dog barking, doors slamming, the auctioneer call of some song.

In the bathroom, I turn out the lights. So I can't see what's in the bag. So I won't know how it's supposed to turn out. In the cramped tight darkness, I stuff a towel in the crack under the door. With the package on my lap, I sit on the toilet and listen.

This is what passes for civilization.

People who would never throw litter from their car will drive past you with their radio blaring. People who'd never blow cigar smoke at you in a crowded restaurant will bellow into their cell phone. They'll shout at each other across the space of a dinner plate.

These people who would never spray herbicides or insecticides will fog the neighborhood with their stereo playing Scottish bag-pipe music. Chinese opera. Country and western.

Outdoors, a bird singing is fine. Patsy Cline is not.

Outdoors, the din of traffic is bad enough. Adding Chopin's Piano Concerto in E Minor is not making the situation any better.

You turn up your music to hide the noise. Other people turn up their music to hide yours. You turn up yours again. Everyone buys a bigger stereo system. This is the arms race of sound. You don't win with a lot of treble.

This isn't about quality. It's about volume.

This isn't about music. This is about winning.

You stomp the competition with the bass line. You rattle windows. You drop the melody line and shout the lyrics. You put in foul language and come down hard on each cussword.

You dominate. This is really about power.

In the dark bathroom, sitting on the toilet, I fingernail the tape open at one end of the package, and what's inside is a square cardboard box, smooth, soft, and furred at the edges, each corner blunt and crushed in. The top lifts off, and what's inside feels like layers of sharp, hard complicated shapes, tiny angles, curves, corners, and points. These I set to one side on the bathroom floor, in the dark. The cardboard box, I put back inside the paper bags. Between the hard, tangled shapes are two sheets of slippery paper. These papers, I put in the bags, too. The bags, I crush and roll and twist into a ball.

All of this I do blind, touching the smooth paper, feeling the layers of hard, branching shapes.

The floor under my shoes, even the toilet seat, shakes a little from the music next door.

Each family with a crib death, you want to tell them to take up a hobby. You'd be surprised just how fast you can close the door on your past. No matter how bad things get, you can still walk away. Learn needlepoint. Make a stained-glass lamp.

I carry the shapes to the kitchen, and in the light they're blue and gray and white. They're brittle-hard plastic. Just tiny shards. Tiny shingles and shutters and bargeboards. Tiny steps and columns and window frames. If it's a house or a hospital, you can't tell. There are little brick walls and little doors. Spread out on the kitchen table, it could be the parts of a school or a church. Without seeing the picture on the box, without the instruction sheets, the tiny gutters and dormers might be for a train station or a lunatic asylum. A factory or a prison.

No matter how you put it together, you're never sure if it's right.

The little pieces, the cupolas and chimneys, they twitch with each beat of noise coming through the floor.

These music-oholics. These calm-ophobics.

No one wants to admit we're addicted to music. That's just not possible. No one's addicted to music and television and radio. We just need more of it, more channels, a larger screen, more volume. We can't bear to be without it, but no, nobody's addicted.

We could turn it off anytime we wanted.

I fit a window frame into a brick wall. With a little brush, the size for fingernail polish, I glue it. The window is the size of a fingernail. The glue smells like hair spray. The smell tastes like oranges and gasoline.

The pattern of the bricks on the wall is as fine as your fingerprint.

Another window fits in place, and I brush on more glue.

The sound shivers through the walls, through the table, through the window frame, and into my finger.

These distraction-oholics. These focus-ophobics.

Old George Orwell got it backward.

Big Brother isn't watching. He's singing and dancing. He's pulling rabbits out of a hat. Big Brother's busy holding your attention every moment you're awake. He's making sure you're always distracted. He's making sure you're fully absorbed.

He's making sure your imagination withers. Until it's as useful as your appendix. He's making sure your attention is always filled.

And this being fed, it's worse than being watched. With the world always filling you, no one has to worry about what's in your mind. With everyone's imagination atrophied, no one will ever be a threat to the world.

I finger open a button on my white shirt and stuff my tie inside. With my chin tucked down tight against the knot of my tie, I tweezer a tiny pane of glass into each window. Using a razor blade, I cut plastic curtains smaller than a postage stamp, blue curtains for the upstairs, yellow for the downstairs. Some curtains left open, some drawn shut, I glue them down.

There are worse things than finding your wife and child dead.

You can watch the world do it. You can watch your wife get old and bored. You can watch your kids discover everything in the world you've tried to save them from. Drugs, divorce, conformity, disease. All the nice clean books, music, television. Distraction.

These people with a dead child, you want to tell them, go ahead. Blame yourself.

There are worse things you can do to the people you love than kill them. The regular way is just to watch the world do it. Just read the newspaper.

The music and laughter eat away at your thoughts. The noise blots them out. All the sound distracts. Your head aches from the glue.

Anymore, no one's mind is their own. You can't concentrate. You can't think. There's always some noise worming in. Singers shouting. Dead people laughing. Actors crying. All these little doses of emotion.

Someone's always spraying the air with their mood.

Their car stereo, broadcasting their grief or joy or anger all over the neighborhood.

One Dutch Colonial mansion, I installed fifty-six windows up-side down and had to throw it out. One twelve-bedroom Tudor castle, I glued the downspouts on the wrong gable ends and melted everything by trying to fix it with a chemical solvent.

This isn't anything new.

Experts in ancient Greek culture say that people back then didn't see their thoughts as belonging to them. When ancient Greeks had a thought, it occurred to them as a god or goddess giving an order. Apollo was telling them to be brave. Athena was telling them to fall in love.

Now people hear a commercial for sour cream potato chips and rush out to buy, but now they call this free will.

At least the ancient Greeks were being honest.

The truth is, even if you read to your wife and child some night. You read them a lullaby. And the next morning, you wake up but your family doesn't. You lie in bed, still curled against your wife. She's still warm but not breathing. Your daughter's not cry-ing. The house is already hectic with traffic and talk radio and steam pounding through the pipes inside the wall. The truth is, you can forget even that day for the moment it takes to make a perfect knot in your tie.

This I know. This is my life.

You might move away, but that's not enough. You'll take up a hobby. You'll bury yourself in work. Change your name. You'll cobble things together. Make order out of chaos. You'll do this each time your foot is healed enough, and you have the money. Organize every detail.

This isn't what a therapist will tell you to do, but it works.

You glue the doors into the walls next. You glue the walls into the foundation. You tweezer together the tiny bits of each chim-ney and let the glue dry while you build the roof. You hang the tiny gutters. Every detail exact. You set the tiny dormers. Hang the shutters. Frame the porch. Seed the lawn. Plant the trees.

Inhale the taste of oranges and gasoline. The smell of hair spray. Lose yourself in each complication. Glue a thread of ivy up one side of the chimney. Your fingers webbed with threads of glue, your fingertips crusted and sticking together.

You tell yourself that noise is what defines silence. Without noise, silence would not be golden. Noise is the exception. Think of deep outer space, the incredible cold and quiet where your wife and kid wait. Silence, not heaven, would be reward enough.

With tweezers, you plant flowers along the foundation.

Your back and neck curve forward over the table. With your ass clenched, your spine's hunched, arching up to a headache at the base of your skull.

You glue the tiny Welcome mat outside the front door. You hook up the tiny lights inside. You glue the mailbox beside the front door. You glue the tiny, tiny milk bottles on the front porch. The tiny folded newspaper.

With everything perfect, exact, meticulous, it must be three or four in the morning, because by now it's quiet. The floor, the ceiling, the walls, are still. The compressor on the refrigerator shuts off, and you can hear the filament buzzing in each lightbulb. You can hear my watch tick. A moth knocks against the kitchen window. You can see your breath, the room is that cold.

You put the batteries in place and flip a little switch, and the tiny windows glow. You set the house on the floor and turn out the kitchen light.

Stand over the house in the dark. From this far away it looks perfect. Perfect and safe and happy. A neat red-brick home. The tiny windows of light shine out on the lawn and trees. The curtains glow, yellow in the baby's room. Blue in your own bedroom.

The trick to forgetting the big picture is to look at everything close-up.

The shortcut to closing a door is to bury yourself in the details.

This is how we must look to God.

As if everything's just fine.

Now take off your shoe, and with your bare foot, stomp. Stomp and keep stomping. No matter how much it hurts, the brittle broken plastic and wood and glass, keep stomping until the downstairs neighbor pounds the ceiling with his fist.

Chapter 4

My second crib death assignment is in a concrete-block housing project on the edge of downtown, the deceased slumped in a high chair in the middle of the afternoon while the baby-sitter cried in the bedroom. The high chair was in the kitchen. Dirty dishes were piled in the sink.

Back in the City Room, Duncan, my editor, asks, "Single or double sink?"

Another detail about Duncan is, when he talks, he spits.

Double, I tell him. Stainless steel. Separate hot and cold knobs, pistol-grip-style with porcelain handles. No spray nozzle.

And Duncan says, "The model of refrigerator?" Little spits of his saliva flash in the office lights.

Amana, I say.

"They have a calendar?" Little touches of Duncan's spit spray my hand, my arm, the side of my face. The spit's cold from the air-conditioning.

The calendar had a painting of an old stone New England mill, I tell him, the waterwheel kind. Sent out by an insurance agent. Written on it was the baby's next appointment at the pediatrician. And the mother's upcoming GED exam. These dates and times and the pediatrician's name are all in my notes.

And Duncan says, "Damn, you're good."

His spit's drying on my skin and lips.

The kitchen floor was gray linoleum. The countertops were pink with black cigarette burns creeping in from the edge. On the counter next to the sink was a library book. *Poems and Rhymes from Around the World.*

The book was shut, and when I set it on its spine, when I let it fall open by itself, hoping it would show how far the reader had cracked the binding, the pages fluttered open to page 27. And I make a pencil mark in the margin.

My editor closes one eye and tilts his head at me. "What," he says, "kind of food dried on the dishes?"

Spaghetti, I say. Canned sauce. The kind with extra mushrooms and garlic. I inventoried the garbage in the bag under the sink.

Two hundred milligrams of salt per serving. One hundred fifty calories of fat. I don't know what I ever expect to find, but like everybody at the scene, it pays to look for a pattern.

Duncan says, "You see this?" and hands me a proof sheet from today's restaurant section. Above the fold, there's an advertisement. It's three columns wide by six inches deep. The top line says:

Attention Patrons of the Treeline Dining Club

The body copy says: "Have you contracted a treatment-resistant form of chronic fatigue syndrome after eating in this establishment? Has this food-borne virus left you unable to work and live a normal life? If so, please call the following number to be part of a class-action lawsuit."

Then there's a phone number with a weird prefix, maybe a cell phone.

Duncan says, "You think there's a story here?" and the page is dotted with his spit.

Here in the City Room, my pager starts to beep. It's the paramedics.

In journalism school, what they want you to be is a camera. A trained, objective, detached professional. Accurate, polished, and observant.

They want you to believe that the news and you are always two separate things. Killers and reporters are mutually exclusive. Whatever the story, this isn't about *you.*

My third baby is in a farmhouse two hours downstate.

My fourth baby is in a condo near a shopping mall.

One paramedic leads me to a back bedroom, saying, "Sorry we called you out on this one." His name is John Nash, and he pulls the sheet off a child in bed, a little boy too perfect, too peaceful, too white to be asleep. Nash says, "This one's almost six years old."

The details about Nash are, he's a big guy in a white uniform. He wears high-top white track shoes and gathers his hair into a little palm tree at the crown of his head.

"We could be working in Hollywood," Nash says. With this kind of clean bloodless death, there's no death agonies, no reverse peristalsis—the death throes where your digestive system works backward and you vomit fecal matter. "You start puking shit," Nash says, "and that's a realistic-type death scene."

What he tells me about crib death is that it occurs most between two and four months after birth. Over 90 percent of deaths occur before six months. Most researchers say that beyond ten months, it's almost impossible. Beyond a year old, the medical examiner calls the cause of death "undetermined." A second death of this nature in a family is considered homicide until proven otherwise.

In the condo, the bedroom walls are painted green. The bed has flannel sheets printed with Scotch terriers. All you can smell is an aquarium full of lizards.

When someone presses a pillow over the face of a child, the medical examiner calls this a "gentle homicide."

My fifth dead child is in a hotel room out by the airport.

With the farmhouse and the condo, there's the book *Poems and Rhymes*... Open to page 27. The same book from the county library with my pencil mark in the margin. In the hotel room, there's no book. It's a double room with the baby curled up in a queen-size bed next to the bed where the parents slept. There's a color television in an armoire, a thirty-six-inch Zenith with fifty-six cable channels and four local. The carpet's brown, the curtains, brown and blue florals. On the bathroom floor is a wet towel spotted with blood and green shaving gel. Somebody didn't flush the toilet.

The bedspreads are dark blue and smell like cigarette smoke.

There's no books anywhere.

I ask if the family has removed anything from the scene, and the officer at the scene says no. But somebody from social services came by to pick up some clothes.

"Oh," he says, "and some library books that were past due."

Chapter 5

The front door swings open, and inside is a woman holding a cell phone to her ear, smiling at me and talking to somebody else.

"Mona," she says into the phone, "you'll have to make this quick. Mr. Streator's just arrived."

She shows me the back of her free hand, the tiny sparkling watch on her wrist, and says, "He's a few minutes early." Her other hand, her long pink fingernails with the tips painted white, with her little black cell phone, these are almost lost in the shining pink cloud of her hair.

Smiling, she says, "Relax, Mona," and her eyes go up and down me. "Brown sport coat," she says, "brown slacks, white shirt." She frowns and winces, "And a blue tie."

The woman tells the phone, "Middle-aged. Five-ten, maybe

one hundred seventy pounds. Caucasian. Brown, green." She winks at me and says, "His hair's a little messy and he didn't shave today, but he looks harmless enough."

She leans forward a little and mouths, *My secretary.*

Into the phone, she says, "What?"

She steps aside and waves me in the door with her free hand. She rolls her eyes until they come around to meet mine and says, "Thank you for your concern, Mona, but I don't think Mr. Streator is here to rape me."

Where we're at is the Gartoller Estate on Walker Ridge Drive, a Georgian-style eight-bedroom house with seven bathrooms, four fireplaces, a breakfast room, a formal dining room, and a fifteen-hundred-square-foot ballroom on the fourth floor. It has a separate six-car garage and a guesthouse. It has an in-ground swimming pool and a fire and intruder alarm system.

Walker Ridge Drive is the kind of neighborhood where they pick up the garbage five days a week. These are the kind of people who appreciate the threat of a good lawsuit, and when you stop by to introduce yourself, they smile and agree.

The Gartoller Estate is beautiful.

These neighbors won't ask you to come inside. They'll stand in their half-open front doors and smile. They'll tell you they really don't know anything about the history of the Gartoller house. It's a house.

If you ask any more, people will glance over your shoulder at the empty street. Then they'll smile again and say, "I can't help you. You really need to call the Realtor."

The sign at 3465 Walker Ridge Drive says Boyle Realty. Shown by appointment only.

At another house, a woman in a maid's uniform answered the door with a little five- or six-year-old girl looking out from behind the maid's black skirt. The maid shook her head, saying she didn't know anything. "You'll have to call the listing agent," she said, "Helen Boyle. It's on the sign."

And the little girl said, "She's a witch."

And the maid closed the door.

Now inside the Gartoller house, Helen Hoover Boyle walks through the echoing, white empty rooms. She's still on her phone as she walks. Her cloud of pink hair, her fitted pink suit, her legs in white stockings, her feet in pink, medium heels. Her lips are gummy with pink lipstick. Her arms sparkle and rattle with gold and pink bracelets, gold chains, charms, and coins.

Enough ornaments for a Christmas tree. Pearls big enough to choke a horse.

Into the phone, she says, "Did you call the people in the Exeter House? They should've run screaming out of there two weeks ago."

She walks through tall double doors, into the next room, then the next.

"Uh-huh," she says. "What do you mean, they're not living there?"

Tall arched windows look out onto a stone terrace. Beyond that is a lawn striped with lawn mower tracks, beyond that a swimming pool.

Into the phone, she says, "You don't spend a million-two on a house and then not live there." Her voice is loud and sharp in these rooms without furniture or carpets.

A small pink and white purse hangs from a long gold chain looped over her shoulder.

Five foot six. A hundred and eighteen pounds. It would be hard to peg her age. She's so thin she must be either dying or rich. Her suit's some kind of nubby sofa fabric, edged with white braid. It's pink, but not shrimp pink. It's more the color of shrimp pâté served on a water cracker with a sprig of parsley and a dollop of caviar. The jacket is tailored tight at her pinched waist and padded square at her shoulders. The skirt is short and snug. The gold buttons, huge.

She's wearing doll clothes.

"No," she says, "Mr. Streator is right here." She lifts her penciled eyebrows and looks at me. "Am I wasting his time?" she says. "I hope not."

Smiling, she tells the phone, "Good. He's shaking his head no."

I have to wonder what about me made her say *middle-aged.*

To tell the truth, I say, I'm not really in the market for a house.

With two pink fingernails over the cell phone, she leans toward me and mouths, *Just one more minute.*

The truth is, I say, I got her name off some records at the county coroner's office. The truth is, I've pored over the forensic records for every local crib death within the past twenty-five years.

And still listening to the phone, without looking at me, she puts the pink fingernails of her free hand against my lapel and keeps them there, pushing just a little. Into the phone, she says, "So what's the problem? Why aren't they living there?"

Judging from her hand, this close-up, she must be in her late thirties or early forties. Still this taxidermied look that passes for beauty above a certain age and income, it's too old for her. Her skin already looks exfoliated, plucked, scruffed, moisturized, and made up until she could be a piece of refinished furniture. Reupholstered in pink. A restoration. Renovated.

Into her cell phone, she shouts, "You're joking! Yes, of course I know what a teardown is!" She says, "That's a historic house!"

Her shoulders draw up, tight against each side of her neck, and then drop. Turning her face away from the phone, she sighs with her eyes closed.

She listens, standing there with her pink shoes and white legs mirrored upside down in the dark wood floor. Reflected deep in the wood, you can see the shadows inside her skirt.

With her free hand cupped over her forehead, she says, "Mona." She says, "We cannot afford to lose that listing. If they replace that house, chances are it will be off the market for good."

Then she's quiet again, listening.

And I have to wonder, since when can't you wear a blue tie with a brown coat?

I duck my head to meet her eyes, saying, Mrs. Boyle? I needed to see her someplace private, outside her office. It's about a story I'm researching.

But she waves her fingers between us. In another second, she walks over to a fireplace and leans into it, bracing her free hand against the mantel, whispering, "When the wrecking ball swings, the neighbors will probably stand and cheer."

A wide doorway opens from this room into another white room with wood floors and a complicated carved ceiling painted white. In the other direction, a doorway opens on a room lined with empty white bookshelves.

"Maybe we could *start* a protest," she says. "We could write some letters to the newspaper."

And I say, I'm from the newspaper.

Her perfume is the smell of leather car seats and old wilted roses and cedar chest lining.

And Helen Hoover Boyle says, "Mona, hold on."

And walking back to me, she says, "What were you saying, Mr. Streator?" Her eyelashes blink once, twice, fast. Waiting. Her eyes are blue.

I'm a reporter from the newspaper.

"The Exeter House is a lovely, *historic* house some people want to tear down," she says, with one hand cupped over her phone. "Seven bedrooms, six thousand square feet. All cherry paneling throughout the first floor."

The empty room is so quiet you can hear a tiny voice on the telephone saying, "Helen?"

Closing her eyes, she says, "It was built in 1935," and she tilts her head back. "It has radiant steam heat, two point eight acres, a tile roof—"

And the tiny voice says, "Helen?"

"—a game room," she says, "a wet bar, a home gym room—"

The problem is, I don't have this much time. All I need to know, I say, is did you ever have a child?

"—a butler's pantry," she says, "a walk-in refrigerator—"

I say, did her son die of crib death about twenty years ago?

Her eyelashes blink once, twice, and she says, "Pardon me?"

I need to know if she read out loud to her son. His name was Patrick. I want to find all existing copies of a certain book.

Holding her phone between her ear and the padded shoulder of her jacket, Helen Boyle snaps open her pink and white purse and takes out a pair of white gloves. Flexing her fingers into each glove, she says, "Mona?"

I need to know if she might still have a copy of this particular book. I'm sorry, but I can't tell her why.

She says, "I'm afraid Mr. Streator will be of no use to us."

I need to know if they did an autopsy on her son.

To me, she smiles. Then she mouths the words *Get out.*

And I raise both my hands, spread open toward her, and start backing away.

I just need to make sure every copy of this book is destroyed.

And she says, "Mona, please call the police."

Chapter 6

In crib deaths, it's standard procedure to assure the parents that they've done nothing wrong. Babies do not smother in their blankets. In the *Journal of Pediatrics*, in a study published in 1945 called "Mechanical Suffocation During Infancy," researchers proved that no baby could smother in bedding. Even the smallest baby, placed facedown on a pillow or mattress, could roll enough to breathe. Even if the child had a slight cold, there's no proof that it's related to the death. There's no proof to link DPT—diphtheria, pertussis, tetanus—inoculations and sudden death. Even if the child had been to the doctor hours before, it still may die.

A cat does not sit on the child and suck out its life.

All we know is, we don't know.

Nash, the paramedic, shows me the purple and red bruises on every child, livor mortis, where the oxygenated hemoglobin settles to the lowest part of the body. The bloody froth leaking from the nose and mouth is what the medical examiner calls purge fluids, a natural part of decomposition. People desperate for an answer will look at livor mortis, at purge fluids, even at diaper rash, and assume child abuse.

The trick to forgetting the big picture is to look at everything close-up.

The shortcut to closing any door is to bury yourself in the little details. The facts. The best part of becoming a reporter is you can hide behind your notebook. Everything is always research.

At the county library, in the juvenile section, the book is back on the shelf, waiting. *Poems and Rhymes from Around the World.* And on page 27 there's a poem. A traditional African poem, the book says. It's eight lines long, and I don't need to copy it. I have it in my notes from the very first baby, the trailer house in the sub-urbs. I tear out the page and put the book back on the shelf.

In the City Room, Duncan says, "How's it going on the dead baby beat?" He says, "I need you to call this number and see what's what," and he hands me a proof sheet from the Lifestyles section, an ad circled in red pen.

Three columns by six inches deep, the copy says:

Attention Patrons of the Meadow Downs
Fitness and Racquet Club

It says: "Have you contracted a flesh-eating fungal infection from the fitness equipment or personal-contact surfaces in their rest rooms? If so, please call the following number to be part of a class-action lawsuit."

At the phone number in question, a man's voice answers, "Deemer, Duke and Diller, Attorneys-at-Law."

The man says, "We'll need your name and address for the

record." Over the phone, he says, "Can you describe your rash? Size. Location. Color. Tissue loss or damage. Be as specific as possible."

There's been a mistake, I say. There's no rash. I say, I'm not calling to be in the lawsuit.

For whatever reason, Helen Hoover Boyle comes to mind.

When I say I'm a reporter for the newspaper, the man says, "I'm sorry, but we're not allowed to discuss the matter until the lawsuit is filed."

I call the racquet club, but they won't talk either. I call the Treeline Dining Club from the earlier ad, but they won't talk. The phone numbers in both ads are the same one. With the weird cell phone prefix. I call it again, and the man's voice says, "Diller, Doom and Duke, Attorneys-at-Law."

And I hang up.

In journalism school, they teach you to start with your most important fact. The inverted pyramid, they call it. Put the who, what, where, when, and why at the top of the article. Then list the lesser facts in descending order. That way, an editor can lop off any length of story without losing anything too important.

All the little details, the smell of the bedspread, the food on the plates, the color of the Christmas tree ornament, that stuff always gets left on the Composing Room floor.

The only pattern in crib death is it tends to increase as the weather cools in the fall. This is the fact my editor wants to lead with in our first installment. Something to panic people. Five babies, five installments. This way we can keep people reading the series for five consecutive Sundays. We can promise to explore the causes and patterns of sudden infant death. We can hold out hope.

Some people still think knowledge is power.

We can guarantee advertisers a highly invested readership. Outside, it's colder already.

Back at the City Room, I ask my editor to do me a little favor.

I think maybe I've found a pattern. It looks as if every parent might have read the same poem out loud to their child the night before it died.

"All five?" he says.

I say, let's try a little experiment.

This is late in the evening, and we're both tired from a long day. We're sitting in his office, and I tell him to listen.

It's an old song about animals going to sleep. It's wistful and sentimental, and my face feels livid and hot with oxygenated hemoglobin while I read the poem out loud under the fluorescent lights, across a desk from my editor with his tie undone and his collar open, leaning back in his chair with his eyes closed. His mouth is open a little, his teeth and his coffee mug are stained the same coffee brown.

What's good is we're alone, and it only takes a minute.

At the end, he opens his eyes and says, "What the fuck was that supposed to mean?"

Duncan, his eyes are green.

His spit lands in little cold specks on my arm, bringing germs, little wet buckshot, bringing viruses. Brown coffee saliva.

I say I don't know. The book calls it a culling song. In some ancient cultures, they sang it to children during famines or droughts, anytime the tribe had outgrown its land. You sing it to warriors crippled in battle and people stricken with disease, anyone you hope will die soon. To end their pain. It's a lullaby.

As far as ethics, what I've learned is a journalist's job isn't to judge the facts. Your job isn't to screen information. Your job is to collect the details. Just what's there. Be an impartial witness. What I know now is someday you won't think twice about calling those parents back on Christmas Eve.

Duncan looks at his watch, then at me, and says, "So what's your experiment?"

Tomorrow, I'll know if there's a causal relationship. A real pattern.

It's just my job to tell the story. I put page 27 through his paper shredder.

Stick and stones may break your bones, but words will never hurt you.

I don't want to explain until I know for sure. This is still a hypothetical situation, so I ask my editor to humor me. I say, "We both need some rest, Duncan." I say, "Maybe we can talk about it in the morning."

Chapter 7

During my first cup of coffee, Henderson walks over from the National desk. Some people grab their coats and head for the elevator. Some grab a magazine and head for the bathroom. Other people duck behind their computer screens and pretend to be on the phone while Henderson stands in the center of the newsroom with his tie loose around his open collar and shouts, "Where the hell is Duncan?"

He yells, "The street edition is going to press, and we need the rest of the damn front page."

Some people just shrug. I pick up my phone.

The details about Henderson are he's got blond hair combed across his forehead. He dropped out of law school. He's an editor on the National desk. He always knows the snow conditions and has a lift pass dangling from every coat he owns. His computer password is "password."

Standing next to my desk, he says, "Streator, is that nasty blue tie the only one you got?"

Holding the phone to my ear, I mouth the word *Interview.* I ask the dial tone, is that B as in "boy"?

Of course I'm not telling anybody about how I read Duncan the poem. I can't call the police. About my theory. I can't explain to Helen Hoover Boyle why I need to ask about her dead son.

My collar feels so tight I have to swallow hard to force any coffee down.

Even if people believed me, the first thing they'd want to know is: *What poem?*

Show it to us. Prove it.

The question isn't, *Would the poem leak out?*

The question is, *How soon would the human race be extinct?*

Here's the power of life and a cold clean bloodless easy death, available to anyone. To everyone. An instant, bloodless, Hollywood death.

Even if I don't tell, how long until *Poems and Rhymes from Around the World* gets into a classroom? How long until page 27, the culling song, gets read to fifty kids before nap time?

How long until it's read over the radio to thousands of people? Until it's set to music? Translated into other languages?

Hell, it doesn't have to be translated to work. Babies don't speak any language.

No one's seen Duncan for three days. Miller thinks Kleine called Duncan at home. Kleine thinks Fillmore called. Everybody's sure somebody else called, but nobody's talked to Duncan. He hasn't answered his e-mail. Carruthers says Duncan didn't bother to call in sick.

Another cup of coffee later, Henderson stops by my desk with a tear sheet from the Leisure section. It's folded to show an ad, three columns by six inches deep. Henderson looks at me tapping my watch and holding it to my ear, and he says, "You see this in the morning edition?"

The ad says:

Attention First-Class Passengers
of Regent-Pacific Airlines

The ad says: "Have you suffered hair loss and/or discomfort from crab lice after coming in contact with airline upholstery, pillows, or blankets? If so, please call the following number to be part of a class-action lawsuit."

Henderson says, "You called about this yet?"

I say, maybe he should just shut up and call.

And Henderson says, "You're Mr. Special Features." He says, "This isn't prison. I ain't your bitch."

This is killing me.

You don't become a reporter because you're good at keeping secrets.

Being a journalist is about telling. It's about bearing the bad news. Spreading the contagion. The biggest story in history. This could be the end of mass media.

The culling song would be a plague unique to the Information Age. Imagine a world where people shun the television, the radio, movies, the Internet, magazines and newspapers. People have to wear earplugs the way they wear condoms and rubber gloves. In the past, nobody worried too much about sex with strangers. Or before that, bites from fleas. Or untreated drinking water. Mosquitoes. Asbestos.

Imagine a plague you catch through your ears.

Sticks and stones will break your bones, but now words can kill, too.

The new death, this plague, can come from anywhere. A song. An overhead announcement. A news bulletin. A sermon. A street musician. You can catch death from a telemarketer. A teacher. An Internet file. A birthday card. A fortune cookie.

A million people might watch a television show, then be dead the next morning because of an advertising jingle.

Imagine the panic.

Imagine a new Dark Age. Exploration and trade routes brought the first plagues from China to Europe. With mass media, we have so many new means of transmission.

Imagine the books burning. And tapes and films and files, radios and televisions, will all go into that same bonfire. All those libraries and bookstores blazing away in the night. People will attack microwave relay stations. People with axes will chop every fiber-optic cable.

Imagine people chanting prayers, singing hymns, to drown out any sound that might bring death. Their hands clamped over their ears, imagine people shunning any song or speech where death could be coded the way maniacs would poison a bottle of aspirin. Any new word. Anything they don't already understand will be suspect, dangerous. Avoided. A quarantine against communication.

And if this was a death spell, an incantation, there had to be others. If *I* know about page 27, someone else must. I'm not the pioneer brain of anything.

How long until someone dissects the culling song and creates another variation, and another, and another? All of them new and improved. Until Oppenheimer invented the atom bomb, it was impossible. Now we have the atom bomb and the hydrogen bomb and the neutron bomb, and people are still expanding on that one idea. We're forced into a new scary paradigm.

If Duncan's dead, he was a necessary casualty. He was my atmospheric nuclear test. He was my Trinity. My Hiroshima.

Still, Palmer from the copy desk is sure Duncan's in Composing.

Jenkins from Composing says Duncan's probably in the art department.

Hawley from Art says he's in the clipping library.

Schott from the library says Duncan's at the copy desk.

Around here, this is what passes for reality.

The kind of security they now have at airports, imagine that kind of crackdown at all libraries, schools, theaters, bookstores, after the culling song leaks out. Anywhere information might be disseminated, you'll find armed guards.

The airwaves will be as empty as a public swimming pool during a polio scare. After that, only a few government broadcasts will air. Only well-scrubbed news and music. After that, any music, books, and movies will be tested on lab animals or volunteer convicts before release to the public.

Instead of surgical masks, people will wear earphones that will give them the soothing constant protection of safe music or birdsongs. People will pay for a supply of "pure" news, a source for "safe" information and entertainment. The way milk and meat and blood are inspected, imagine books and music and movies being filtered and homogenized. Certified. Approved for consumption.

People will be happy to give up most of their culture for the assurance that the tiny bit that comes through is safe and clean.

White noise.

Imagine a world of silence where any sound loud enough or long enough to harbor a deadly poem would be banned. No more motorcycles, lawn mowers, jet planes, electric blenders, hair dryers. A world where people are afraid to listen, afraid they'll hear something behind the din of traffic. Some toxic words buried in the loud music playing next door. Imagine a higher and higher resistance to language. No one talks because no one dares to listen.

The deaf shall inherit the earth.

And the illiterate. The isolated. Imagine a world of hermits.

Another cup of coffee, and I have to piss like a bastard. Henderson from National catches me washing my hands in the men's room and says something.

It could be anything.

Drying my hands under the blower, I yell I can't hear him.

"Duncan!" Henderson yells. Over the sound of water and the hand dryer, he yells, "We have two dead bodies in a hotel suite, and we don't know if it's news or not. We need Duncan to make the call."

I guess that's what he says. There's so much noise.

In the mirror, I check my tie and finger-comb my hair. In one breath, with Henderson reflected next to me, I could race through the culling song, and he'd be out of my life by tonight. Him and Duncan. Dead. It would be that easy.

Instead, I ask if it's okay to wear a blue tie with a brown jacket.

Chapter 8

When the first paramedic arrived on the scene, the first action he took was to call his stockbroker. This paramedic, my friend John Nash, sized up the situation in suite 17F of the Pressman Hotel and put in a sell order for all his shares of Stuart Western Technologies.

"They can fire me, okay," Nash says, "but in the three minutes I made that call, those two in the bed weren't getting any deader."

The next call he makes is to me, asking if I've got fifty bucks for him to find out a few extra facts. He says if I got shares of Stuart Western to dump them and then get my ass over to this bar on Third, near the hospital.

"Christ," Nash says over the phone, "this woman was beautiful. If Turner hadn't been there, Turner my partner, I don't know." And he hangs up.

According to the ticker, shares of Stuart Western Tech are already sliding into the toilet. Already the news must be out about Baker Lewis Stuart, the company's founder, and his new wife, Penny Price Stuart.

Last night, the Stuarts had dinner at seven o'clock at Chez Chef. This is all easy enough to bribe out of the hotel concierge. According to their waiter, one had the salmon risotto, the other had Portabello mushrooms. Looking at the check, he said, you can't tell who had what. They drank a bottle of pinot noir. Somebody had cheesecake for dessert. Both of them had coffee.

At nine, they drove to an after-hours party at the Chambers Gallery, where witnesses told police the couple talked to several people including the gallery owner and the architect of their new house. They each had another glass of some jug wine.

At ten-thirty, they returned to the Pressman Hotel, where they'd been staying in suite 17F for almost a month since their wedding.

The hotel operator says they made several phone calls between ten-thirty and midnight. At twelve-fifteen, they called the front desk and asked for an eight o'clock wake-up call. A desk clerk confirms that they used the television remote control to order a pornographic movie.

At nine the next morning, the maid found them dead.

"Embolism, if you ask me," Nash says. "You eat a girl out and you blow some air inside her, or if you fuck her too hard, either way you can force air into her bloodstream and the bubble goes right to her heart."

Nash is heavy. A big guy wearing a heavy coat over his white uniform, he's wearing his white track shoes and standing at the bar when I get there. Both elbows on the bar, he's eating a steak sandwich on a kaiser roll with mustard and mayo squeezing out of the far end. He's drinking a cup of black coffee. His greasy hair is pulled into a black palm tree on top of his head.

And I say, so?

I ask, was the place ransacked?

Nash is just chewing, his big jaw going around and around. He holds the sandwich in both hands but stares past it at the plate full of mess, dill pickles and potato chips.

I ask, did he smell anything in the hotel room?

He says, "Newlyweds like they were, I figure he fucks her to death, and then has himself a heart attack. Five bucks says they open her and find air in her heart."

I ask, did he at least star-69 their telephone to find out who'd called last?

And Nash says, "No can do. Not on a hotel phone."

I say, I want more for my fifty bucks than just his drooling over a dead body.

"You'da been drooling, too," he says. "Damn, she was a looker."

I ask, were there valuables—watches, wallets, jewelry—left at the scene?

He says, "Still warm, too, under the covers. Warm enough. No death agonies. Nothing."

His big jaw goes around and around, slower now as he stares down at nothing in particular.

"If you could have any woman you wanted," he says, "if you could have her any way you wanted, wouldn't you do it?"

I say, what he's talking about is rape.

"Not," he says, "if she's dead." And he crunches down on a potato chip in his mouth. "If I'd been alone, alone and had a rubber . . . ," he says through the food. "No way would I let the medical examiner find my DNA at the scene."

Then he's talking about murder.

"Not if somebody else kills her," Nash says, and looks at me. "Or kills *him*. The husband had a fine-looking ass, if that's what floats your boat. No leakage. No livor mortis. No skin slippage. Nothing."

How he can talk this way and still eat, I don't know.

He says, "Both of them naked. A big wet spot on the mattress, right between them. Yeah, they did it. Did it and died." Nash chews his sandwich and says, "Seeing her there, she was better-looking than any piece of tail I've ever had."

If Nash knew the culling song, there wouldn't be a woman left alive. Alive or a virgin.

If Duncan is dead, I hope it's not Nash who responds to the call. Maybe this time with a rubber. Maybe they sell them in the bathroom here.

Since he had such a good look, I ask if he saw any bruises, bites, beestings, needle marks, anything.

"It's nothing like that," he says.

A suicide note?

"Nope. No apparent cause of death," he says.

Nash turns the sandwich around in his hands and licks the mustard and mayo leaked out the end. He says, "You remember Jeffrey Dahmer." Nash licks and says, "He didn't set out to kill so many people. He just thought you could drill a hole in somebody's skull, pour in some drain cleaner, and make them your sex zombie. Dahmer just wanted to be getting more."

So what do I get for my fifty bucks?

"A name's all I got," he says.

I give him two twenties and a ten.

With his teeth, he pulls a slice of steak out of the sandwich. The meat hangs against his chin before he tosses his head back to flip it into his mouth. Chewing, he says, "Yeah, I'm a pig," and his breath is nothing but mustard. He says, "The last person to talk to them, their call history on both their cell phones, it said her name is Helen Hoover Boyle."

He says, "You dump that stock like I told you?"

Chapter 9

It's the same William and Mary bureau cabinet. According to the note card taped to the front, it's black lacquered pine with Persian scenes in silver gilt, round bun feet, and the pediment done up in a pile of carved curls and shells. It has to be the same cabinet. We'd turned right here, walking down a tight corridor of armoires, then turned right again at a Regency press cupboard, then left at a Federal sofa, but here we are again.

Helen Hoover Boyle puts her finger against the silver gilt, the tarnished men and women of Persian court life, and says, "I have no idea what you're talking about."

She killed Baker and Penny Stuart. She called them on their cell phones sometime the day before they died. She read them each the culling song.

"You think I killed those unfortunate people by *singing* to them?" she says. Her suit is yellow today, but her hair's still big and pink. Her shoes are yellow, but her neck's still hung with gold chains and beads. Her cheeks look pink and soft with too much powder.

It didn't take much digging to find out the Stuarts were the people who'd bought a house on Exeter Drive. A lovely *historic* house with seven bedrooms and cherry paneling throughout the first floor. A house they planned to tear down and replace. A plan that infuriated Helen Hoover Boyle.

"Oh, Mr. Streator," she says. "If you could just hear yourself."

From where we're standing, a tight corridor of furniture stretches a few yards in every direction. Beyond that, each corridor turns or branches into more corridors, armoires squeezed side by side, sideboards wedged together. Anything short, armchairs or sofas or tables, only lets you see through to the next corridor of hutches, the next wall of grandfather clocks, enameled screens, Georgian secretaries.

This is where she suggested we meet, where we could talk in private, one of those warehouse antique stores. In this maze of furniture, we keep meeting the same William and Mary bureau cabinet, then the same Regency press cupboard. We're going in circles. We're lost.

And Helen Boyle says, "Have you told anyone else about your killer song?"

Only my editor.

"And what did your editor say?"

I think he's dead.

And she says, "What a surprise." She says, "You must feel terrible."

Above us, crystal chandeliers hang at different heights, all of them cloudy and gray as powdered wigs. Frayed wires twist where their chains hook onto each roof beam. The severed wires, the dusty dead lightbulbs. Each chandelier is just another ancient aristocratic head cut off and hanging upside down. Above everything arches the warehouse roof, a lot of bow trusses supporting corrugated steel.

"Just follow me," Helen Boyle says. "Isn't moss supposed to grow only on the north side of an armoire?"

She wets two fingers in her mouth and holds them up.

The Rococo vitrines, the Jacobean bookcases, the Gothic Revival highboys, all carved and varnished, the French Provincial wardrobes, crowd around us. The Edwardian walnut curio cabinets, the Victorian pier mirrors, the Renaissance Revival chifforobes. The walnut and mahogany, ebony and oak. The melon bulb legs and cabriole legs and linenfold panels. Past the point where any corridor turns, there's just more. Queen Anne chiffoniers. More bird's-eye maple. Mother-of-pearl inlay and gilded bronze ormolu.

Our footsteps echo against the concrete floor. The steel roof hums with rain.

And she says, "Don't you feel, somehow, buried in history?"

With her pink fingernails, from out of her yellow and white bag, she takes a ring of keys. She makes a fist around the keys so only the longest and sharpest juts out between her fingers.

"Do you realize that anything you can do in your lifetime will be meaningless a hundred years from now?" she says. "Do you think, a century from now, that anyone will even remember the Stuarts?"

She looks from one polished surface to the next, tabletops, dressers, doors, all with her reflection floating across them.

"People die," she says. "People tear down houses. But furniture, fine, beautiful furniture, it just goes on and on, surviving everything."

She says, "Armoires are the cockroaches of our culture."

And without breaking her stride, she drags the steel point of the key across the polished walnut face of a cabinet. The sound is as quiet as anything sharp slashing something soft. The scar is deep and shows the raw cheap pine under the veneer.

She stops in front of a wardrobe with beveled-glass doors.

"Think of all the generations of women who looked in that mirror," she says. "They took it home. They aged in that mirror. They died, all those beautiful young women, but here's the wardrobe, worth more now than ever. A parasite surviving the host. A big fat predator looking for its next meal."

In this maze of antiques, she says, are the ghosts of everyone who has ever owned this furniture. Everyone rich and successful enough to prove it. All of their talent and intelligence and beauty, outlived by decorative junk. All the success and accomplishment this furniture was supposed to represent, it's all vanished.

She says, "In the vast scheme of things, does it really matter how the Stuarts died?"

I ask, how did she find out about the culling spell? Was it because her son, Patrick, died?

And she just keeps walking, trailing her fingers along the carved edges, the polished surfaces, marring the knobs and smearing the mirrors.

It didn't take much digging to find out how her husband died. A year after Patrick, he was found in bed, dead without a mark, without a suicide note, without a cause.

And Helen Boyle says, "How was your editor found?"

Out of her yellow and white purse, she takes a gleaming silver little pair of pliers and a screwdriver, so clean and exact they could be used in surgery. She opens the door on a vast carved and polished armoire and says, "Hold this steady for me, please."

I hold the door and she's busy on the inside for a moment until the door's latch and handle fall free and hit the floor at my feet.

A minute later, and she has the door handles, and the gilded bronze ormolu, she's taken everything metal except the hinges and put them in her purse. Stripped, the armoire looks crippled, blind, castrated, mutilated.

And I ask, why is she doing this?

"Because I love this piece," she says. "But I'm not going to be another one of its victims."

She closes the doors and puts her tools away in her purse.

"I'll come back for it after they cut the price down to what it cost when it was new," she says. "I love it, but I'll only have it on my own terms."

We walk a few steps more, and the corridor breaks into a forest of hall trees and hat racks, umbrella stands and coat racks. In the distance beyond that is another wall of breakfronts and armoires.

"Elizabethan," she says, touching each piece. "Tudor . . . Eastlake . . . Stickley . . ."

When someone takes two old pieces, say a mirror and a dresser, and fastens them together, she explains that experts call the product a "married" piece. As an antique, it's considered worthless.

When someone takes two pieces apart, say a buffet and a hutch, and sells them separately, experts call the pieces "divorced."

"And again," she says, "they're worthless."

I say how I've been trying to find every copy of the poems book. I say how important it is that no one ever discovers the spell. After what happened to Duncan, I swear I'm going to burn all my notes and forget I ever knew the culling spell.

"And what if you can't forget it?" she says. "What if it stays in your head, repeating itself like one of those silly advertising songs? What if it's always there, like a loaded gun waiting for someone to annoy you?"

I won't use it.

"Hypothetically speaking, of course," she says, "what if I used to swear the same thing? Me. A woman you're saying accidentally killed her own child and husband, someone who's been tortured by the power of this curse. If someone like me eventually began using the song, what makes you think that you won't?"

I just won't.

"Of course you won't," she says, and then laughs without making a sound. She turns right, past a Biedermeier credenza, fast, then turns again past an Art Nouveau console, and for a minute she's out of sight.

I hurry to catch up, still lost, saying, if we're going to find our way out of this, I think we need to stay together.

Just ahead of us is a William and Mary bureau cabinet. Black lacquered pine with Persian scenes in silver gilt, round bun feet, and the pediment done up in a pile of carved curls and shells. And leading me deeper into the thicket of cabinets and closets and breakfronts and highboys, the rocking chairs and hall trees and bookcases, Helen Hoover Boyle says she needs to tell me a little story.

Chapter 10

Back at the newsroom, everybody's quiet. People are whispering around the coffeemaker. People are listening with their mouths hanging open. Nobody's crying.

Henderson catches me hanging my jacket and says, "You call Regent-Pacific Airlines about their crab lice?"

And I say, nobody's saying anything until a suit is filed.

And Henderson says, "Just so you know, you report to me now." He says, "Duncan's not just irresponsible. It turns out he's dead."

Dead in bed without a mark. No suicide note, no cause of death. His landlord found him and called the paramedics.

And I ask, any sign he was sodomized?

And Henderson jerks his head back just a trace and says, "Say what?"

Did somebody fuck him?

"God, no," Henderson says. "Why would you ask such a thing?"

And I say, no reason.

At least Duncan wasn't somebody's dead-body sex doll.

I say, if anybody needs me, I'll be in the clipping library. There's some facts I need to check. Just a few years of newspaper stories I need to read. A few spools of microfilm to run through.

And Henderson calls after me, "Don't go far. Just because Duncan's dead, that don't mean you're off the dead baby beat."

Sticks and stones may break your bones, but watch out for those damn words.

According to the microfilm, in 1983, in Vienna, Austria, a twenty-three-year-old nurse's aide gave an overdose of morphine to an old woman who was begging to die.

The seventy-seven-year-old woman died, and the aide, Waltraud Wagner, found she loved having the power of life and death.

It's all here in spool after spool of microfilm. Just the facts.

At first it was just to help dying patients. She worked in an enormous hospital for the elderly and chronically ill. People lingered there, wanting to die. Besides morphine, the young woman invented what she called her water cure. To relieve suffering, you just pinch the patient's nose shut. You depress the tongue, and you pour water down the throat. Death is slow torture, but old people are always found dead with water collected in their lungs.

The young woman called herself an angel.

It looked very natural.

It was a noble, heroic deed that Wagner was doing.

She was the ultimate end to suffering and misery. She was gentle and caring and sensitive, and she only took those who begged to die. She was the angel of death.

By 1987, there were three more angels. All four aides worked the night shift. By now the hospital was nicknamed the Death Pavilion.

Instead of ending suffering, the four women began to give their water cure to patients who snored or wet the bed or refused to take medication or buzzed the nurse's station late at night. Any petty annoyance, and the patient died the next night. Anytime a patient complained about anything, Waltraud Wagner would say, "This one gets a ticket to God," and glug, glug, glug.

"The ones who got on my nerves," she told authorities, "were dispatched directly to a free bed with the good Lord."

In 1989, an old woman called Wagner a common slut, and got the water cure. Afterward, the angels were drinking in a tavern, laughing and mimicking the old woman's convulsions and the look on her face. A doctor sitting nearby overheard.

By then, the Vienna health authorities estimate that almost three hundred people had been cured. Wagner got life in prison. The other angels got lesser sentences.

"We could decide whether these old fogies lived or died," Wagner said at her trial. "Their ticket to God was long overdue in any case."

The story Helen Hoover Boyle told me is true.

Power corrupts. And absolute power corrupts absolutely.

So just relax, Helen Boyle told me, and just enjoy the ride.

She said, "Even absolute corruption has its perks."

She said to think of all the people you'd like out of your life. Think of all the loose ends you could tie up. The revenge. Think how easy it would be.

And still echoing in my head was Nash. Nash was there, drooling over the idea of any woman, anywhere, cooperative and beautiful for at least a few hours before things start to cool down and fall apart.

"Tell me," he said, "how would that be different than most love relationships?"

Anyone and everyone could become your next sex zombie.

But just because this Austrian nurse and Helen Boyle and John Nash can't control themselves, that doesn't mean I'll become a reckless, impulsive killer.

Henderson comes to the library doorway and shouts, "Streator! Did you turn off your pager? We just got a call about another cold baby."

The editor is dead, long live the editor. Here's the new boss, same as the old boss.

And, sure, the world just might be a better place without certain people. Yeah, the world could be just perfect, with a little trimming here and there. A little housecleaning. Some unnatural selection.

But, no, I'm never going to use the culling song again.

Never again.

But even if I did use it, I wouldn't use it for revenge.

I wouldn't use it for convenience.

I certainly wouldn't use it for sex.

No, I'd only ever use it for good.

And Henderson yells, "Streator! Did you ever call about the first-class crab lice? Did you call about the health club's butt-eating fungus? You need to pester those people at the Treeline or you'll never get anything."

And fast as a flinch, me flinching the other way down the hall, the culling song spools through my head while I grab my coat and head out the door.

But, no, I'm never going to use it. That's that. I'm just not. Ever.

Chapter 11

These noise-oholics. These quiet-ophobics.

There's the stomp and stomp and stomp of a drum coming down through the ceiling. Through the walls, you hear the laughter and applause of dead people.

Even in the bathroom, even taking a shower, you can hear talk radio over the hiss of the showerhead, the splash of water in the tub and blasting against the plastic curtain. It's not that you want everybody dead, but it would be nice to unleash the culling spell on the world. Just to enjoy the fear. After people outlawed loud sounds, any sounds that could harbor a spell, any music or noise that might mask a deadly poem, after that the world would be silent. Dangerous and frightened, but silent.

The tile beats a tiny rhythm under my fingertips. The bathtub vibrates with shouts coming through the floor. Either a prehistoric flying dinosaur awakened by a nuclear test is about to destroy the people downstairs or their television's too loud.

In a world where vows are worthless. Where making a pledge means nothing. Where promises are made to be broken, it would be nice to see words come back into power.

In a world where the culling song was common knowledge, there would be sound blackouts. Like during wartime, wardens would patrol. But instead of hunting for light, they'd listen for noise and tell people to shut up. The way governments look for air and water pollution, these same governments would pinpoint anything above a whisper, then make an arrest. There would be helicopters, special muffled helicopters, of course, to search for noise the way they search for marijuana now. People would tiptoe around in rubber-soled shoes. Informers would listen at every keyhole.

It would be a dangerous, frightened world, but at least you could sleep with your windows open. It would be a world where each word was worth a thousand pictures.

It's hard to say if that world would be any worse than this, the pounding music, the roar of television, the squawk of radio.

Maybe without Big Brother filling us, people could think.

The upside is maybe our minds would become our own.

It's harmless so I say the first line of the culling poem. There's no one here to kill. No way could anyone hear it.

And Helen Hoover Boyle is right. I haven't forgot it. The first word generates the second. The first line generates the next. My voice booms as big as an opera. The words thunder with the deep rolling sound of a bowling alley. The thunder echoes against the tile and linoleum.

In my big opera voice, the culling song doesn't sound silly the way it did in Duncan's office. It sounds heavy and rich. It's the sound of doom. It's the doom of my upstairs neighbor. It's my end to his life, and I've said the whole poem.

Even wet, the hair's bristling on the back of my neck. My breathing's stopped.

And, nothing.

From upstairs, there's the stomp of music. From every direction, there's radio and television talk, tiny gunshots, laughter, bombs, sirens. A dog barks. This is what passes for prime time.

I turn off the water. I shake my hair. I pull back the shower curtain and reach for a towel. And then I see it.

The vent.

The air shaft, it connects every apartment. The vent, it's always open. It carries steam from the bathrooms, cooking smells from the kitchens. It carries every sound.

Dripping on the bathroom floor, I just stare at the vent.

It could be I've just killed the whole building.

Chapter 12

Nash is at the bar on Third, eating onion dip with his fingers. He sticks two shiny fingers into his mouth, sucking so hard his cheeks cave in. He pulls the fingers out and pinches some more onion dip out of a plastic tub.

I ask if that's breakfast.

"You got a question," he says, "you need to show me the money first." And he puts the fingers in his mouth.

On the other side of Nash, down the bar is some young guy with sideburns, wearing a good pin-striped suit. Next to him is a gal, standing on the bar rail so she can kiss him. He tosses the cherry from his cocktail into his mouth. They kiss. Then she's chewing. The radio behind the bar is still announcing the school lunch menus.

Nash keeps turning his head to watch them.

This is what passes for love.

I put a ten-dollar bill on the bar.

His fingers still in his mouth, his eyes look down at it. Then his eyebrows come up.

I ask, did anybody die in my building last night?

It's the apartments at Seventeenth and Loomis Place. The Loomis Place Apartments, eight stories, a kind of kidney-colored brick. Maybe somebody on the fifth floor? Near the back? A young guy. This morning, there's a weird stain on my ceiling.

The sideburns guy, his cell phone starts ringing.

And Nash pulls his fingers out, his lips dragged out around them in a tight pucker. Nash looks at his fingernails, close-up, cross-eyed.

The dead guy was into drugs, I tell him. A lot of people in that building are into drugs. I ask if there were any other dead people there. By any chance did a whole bunch of people die in the Loomis Place Apartments last night?

And the sideburns guy grabs the gal by a handful of hair and pulls her away from his mouth. With his other hand, he takes a phone from inside his coat and flips it open, saying, "Hello?"

I say, they'd all be found with no apparent cause of death.

Nash stirs a finger around in the onion dip and says, "That your building?"

Yeah, I already said that.

Still holding the gal by her hair, talking into the phone, the sideburns guy says, "No, honey." He says, "I'm at the doctor's office right now, and it doesn't look very good."

The gal closes her eyes. She arches her neck back and grinds her hair into his hand.

And the sideburns guy says, "No, it looks like it's metastasized." He says, "No, I'm okay."

The gal opens her eyes.

He winks at her.

She smiles.

And the sideburns guy says, "That means a lot right now. I love you, too."

He hangs up, and he pulls the gal's face into his.

And Nash takes the ten off the bar and stuffs it into his pocket. He says, "Nope. I didn't hear anything."

The gal, her feet slip off the bar rail, and she laughs. She steps back up and says, "Was that her?"

And the sideburns guy says, "No."

And without me trying, it happens. Me just looking at the sideburns guy, the song flits through my head. The song, my voice in the shower, the voice of doom, it echoes inside me. As fast as a reflex. As fast as a sneeze, it happens.

Nash, his breath is nothing but onions, he says, "It sounds kind of funny, you asking that." He puts his stirring finger into his mouth.

And the gal down the bar says, "Marty?"

And the sideburns guy leaning against the bar slides to the floor.

Nash turns to look.

The gal's kneeling next to the guy on the floor, her hands spread open just above, but not quite touching, his pin-striped lapels, and she says, "Marty?" Her fingernails are painted sparkling purple. Her purple lipstick is smeared all around the guy's mouth.

And maybe the guy's really sick. Maybe he's choked on a cherry. Maybe I didn't just make another kill.

The gal looks up at Nash and me, her face glossy with tears, and says, "Does one of you know CPR?"

Nash puts his fingers back in the onion dip, and I step over the body, past the gal, pulling on my coat, headed for the door.

Chapter 13

Back in the newsroom, Wilson from the International desk wants to know if I've seen Henderson today. Baker from the Books desk says Henderson didn't call in sick, and he doesn't answer his phone at home. Oliphant from the Special Features desk says, "Streator, you seen this?"

He hands me a tear sheet, an ad that says:

Attention Patrons of the French Salon

It says: "Have you experienced severe bleeding and scarring as a result of recent facials?"

The phone number is one I haven't seen before, and when I dial, a woman answers: "Doogan, Diller and Dunne, Attorneys-at-Law," she says.

And I hang up.

Oliphant stands by my desk and says, "While you're here, say something nice about Duncan." They're putting together a feature, he says, a tribute to Duncan, a nice portrait and a summary of his career, and they need people to think up good quotes. Somebody in Art is using the photo from Duncan's employee badge to paint the portrait. "Only smiling," Oliphant says. "Smiling and more like a human being."

Before that, walking from the bar on Third, back to work, I counted my steps. To keep my mind busy, I counted 276 steps until a guy wearing a black leather trench coat shoves past me at a street corner, saying, "Wake up, asshole. The sign says, 'Walk.' "

Hitting me as sudden as a yawn, me glaring at the guy's black leather back, the culling song loops through my head.

Still crossing the street, the guy in the trench coat lifts his foot to step over the far curb, but doesn't clear it. His toe kicks into the curb halfway up, and he pitches forward onto the sidewalk, flat on his forehead. It's the sound of dropping an egg on the kitchen floor, only a really big, big egg full of blood and brains. His arms lie straight down at his sides. The toes of his black wing tips hang off the curb a little, over the gutter.

I step past him, counting 277, counting 278, counting 279 . . .

A block from the newspaper, a sawhorse barricade blocks the sidewalk. A police officer in a blue uniform stands on the other side shaking his head. "You have to go back and cross the street. This sidewalk's closed." He says, "They're shooting a movie up the block."

Hitting me as fast as a cramp, me scowling at his badge, the eight lines of the song run through my mind.

The officer's eyes roll up until only the whites show. One gloved hand gets halfway to his chest, and his knees fold. His chin comes down on the top edge of the barricade so hard you can hear his teeth click together. Something pink flies out. It's the tip of his tongue.

Counting 345, counting 346, counting 347, I haul one leg then the other over the barricade and keep walking.

A woman with a walkie-talkie in one hand steps into my path, one arm straight out in front of her, her hand reaching to stop me. The moment before her hand should grab my arm, her eyes roll over and her lips drop open. A thread of drool slips out one corner of her slack mouth, and she falls through my path, her walkie-talkie saying, "Jeanie? Jean? Stand by."

The last words of the culling song trail through my head.

Counting 359, counting 360, counting 361, I keep walking as people rush past me in the other direction. A woman with a light meter hanging on a cord around her neck says, "Did somebody call an ambulance?"

People dressed in rags, wearing thick makeup and drinking water out of little blue-glass bottles, they stand in front of shopping carts piled with trash under big lights and reflectors, stretching their necks to see where I've been. The curb is lined with big trailers and motor homes with the smell of diesel generators running in between them. Paper cups half full of coffee are sitting everywhere.

Counting 378, counting 379, counting 380, I step over the barricade on the far side and keep walking. It takes 412 steps to get to the newsroom. In the elevator, on the way up, there's already too many people crowded in. On the fifth floor, another man tries to shoulder his way into the car.

Sudden as breaking a sweat, me squeezed against the back of the elevator, my mind spits out the culling song so hard my lips move with each word.

The man looks at us all, and seems to step back in slow motion. Before we see him hit the floor, the doors are closed and we're going up.

In the newsroom, Henderson is missing. Oliphant comes over while I'm dialing my phone. He tells me about the tribute to

Duncan. Asks for quotes. He shows me the ad on the tear sheet. The ad about the French Salon, the bleeding facials. Oliphant asks where my next installment is on the crib death series.

The phone in my hand, I'm counting 435, counting 436, counting 437 . . .

To him, I say to just not piss me off.

A woman's voice on the phone says, "Helen Boyle Realty. May I help you?"

And Oliphant says, "Have you tried counting to 10?"

The details about Oliphant are he's fat, and his hands sweated brown handprints on the tear sheet he shows me. His computer password is "password."

And I say, I passed 10 a long time ago.

And the voice on the phone says, "Hello?"

With my hand over the phone, I tell Oliphant there must be a virus going around. That's probably why Henderson's gone. I'm going home, but I promise to file my story from there.

Oliphant mouths the words *Four o'clock deadline*, and he taps the face of his wristwatch.

And into the phone, I ask, is Helen Hoover Boyle in the office? I say, my name's Streator, and I need to see her right away.

I'm counting 489, counting 490, counting 491 . . .

The voice says, "Will she know what this is regarding?"

Yeah, I say, but she'll pretend she doesn't.

I say, she needs to stop me before I kill again.

And Oliphant backs away a couple steps before he breaks eye contact and heads toward Special Features. I'm counting 542, counting 543 . . .

On my way to the real estate office, I ask the cab to wait in front of my apartment building while I run upstairs.

The brown stain on my ceiling is bigger. It's maybe as big around as a tire, only now the stain has arms and legs.

Back in the cab, I try to buckle my seat belt, but it's adjusted too small. It cuts into me, my gut riding on top of it, and I hear

Helen Hoover Boyle saying, "Middle-aged. Five-ten, maybe one hundred seventy pounds. Caucasian. Brown, green." I see her under her bubble of pink hair, winking at me.

I tell the driver the address for the real estate office, and I tell him that he can drive as fast as he wants, but just not to piss me off.

The details about the cab are it stinks. The seat is black and sticky. It's a cab.

I say, I have a little problem with anger.

The driver looks at me in his rearview mirror and says, "You should maybe get some anger management classes."

And I'm counting 578, counting 579, counting 580 . . .

Chapter 14

According to *Architectural Digest*, big mansions surrounded by vast estate gardens and thoroughbred horse farms are really good places to live. According to *Town & Country*, strands of fat pearls are lustrous. According to *Travel & Leisure*, a private yacht anchored in the sunny Mediterranean is relaxing.

In the waiting room of the Helen Boyle Real Estate Agency, this is what passes as a big news flash. A real scoop.

On the coffee table, there's copies of all these high-end magazines. There's a humpbacked Chesterfield couch upholstered in striped pink silk. The sofa table behind it has long lion legs, their claws gripping glass balls. You have to wonder how much of this furniture came here stripped of its hardware, its drawer pulls and metal details. Sold as junk, it came here and Helen Hoover Boyle put it back together.

A young woman, half my age, sits behind a carved Louis XIV desk, staring at a clock radio on the desk. Her desk plate says, *Mona Sabbat*. Next to the clock radio is a police scanner crackling with static.

On the clock radio, an older woman is yelling at a younger woman. It seems the younger woman has gotten pregnant out of wedlock so the older woman is calling her a slut and a whore. A stupid whore, the older woman says, since the slut spread her legs without even getting paid.

The woman at the desk, this Mona person, turns off the police scanner and says, "I hope you don't mind. I love this show."

These media-holics. These quiet-ophobics.

On the clock radio, the older woman tells the slut to give her baby up for adoption unless she wants to ruin its future. She tells the slut to grow up and finish her degree in microbiology, then get married, but not have any more sex until then.

Mona Sabbat takes a brown paper bag from under the desk and takes out something wrapped in foil. She picks the foil open at one end and you can smell garlic and marigolds.

On the clock radio, the pregnant slut just cries and cries.

Sticks and stones may break your bones, but words can hurt like hell.

According to an article in *Town & Country*, beautifully hand-written personal correspondence on luxurious stationery is once again very in, in, in. In a copy of *Estate* magazine, there's an advertisement that says:

Attention Patrons of the Bridle Mountain
Riding and Polo Club

It says: "Have you contracted a parasitic skin infection from a mount?"

The phone number is one I haven't seen before.

The radio woman tells the slut to stop crying.

Here's Big Brother, singing and dancing, force-feeding you so your mind never gets hungry enough to think.

Mona Sabbat puts both elbows on her desk, and cradles her lunch in her hands, leaning close to the radio. The phone rings, and she answers it, saying, "Helen Boyle Realty. The Right Home Every Time." She says, "Sorry, Oyster, Dr. Sara's on." She says, "I'll see you at the ritual."

The radio woman calls the crying slut a bitch.

The cover of *First Class* magazine says: "Sable, the Justifiable Homicide."

And fast as a hiccup, me only half listening to the radio, me half reading, the culling song goes through my head.

From the clock radio, all you can hear is the slut sobbing and sobbing.

Instead of the older woman, there's silence. Sweet, golden silence. Too perfect to be anyone left alive.

The slut draws a long breath and asks, "Dr. Sara?" She says, "Dr. Sara, are you still there?"

And a deep voice comes on, saying the *Dr. Sara Lowenstein Show* is temporarily experiencing some technical difficulties. The deep voice apologizes. A moment later, dance music starts up.

The cover of *Manor-Born* magazine says: "Diamonds Go Casual!"

I put my face in my hands and groan.

The Mona person peels the foil back from her lunch and takes another bite. She turns off the radio and says, "Bummer."

On the backs of her hands, rusty brown henna designs trail down her fingers, her fingers and thumbs lumpy with silver rings. A lot of silver chains loop around her neck and disappear into her orange dress. On her chest, the crinkled orange fabric of her dress is bumpy from all the pendants hanging underneath. Her hair is a thousand coils and dreadlocks of red and black pinned up over silver filigree earrings. Her eyes look amber. Her fingernails, black.

I ask if she's worked here long.

"You mean," she says, "in earth time?" And she takes a paperback from a drawer in her desk. She uncaps a bright yellow highlighter and opens the book.

I ask if Mrs. Boyle ever talks about poetry.

And Mona says, "You mean Helen?"

Yeah, does she ever recite poetry? In her office, does she ever call people on the phone and read any poems to them?

"Don't get me wrong," Mona says, "but Mrs. Boyle's way too much into the money side of everything. You know?"

I have to start counting 1, counting 2 . . .

"It's like this," she says. "When traffic's bad, Mrs. Boyle makes me drive home with her—just so's she can use the car-pool lane. Then I have to take three buses to get home myself. You know?"

I'm counting 4, counting 5 . . .

She says, "One time, we had this great sharing about the power of crystal. It's like we were finally connecting on some level, only it turns out we were talking about two totally different realities."

Then I'm on my feet. Unfolding a sheet of paper from my back pocket, I show her the poem and ask if it looks familiar.

Highlighted in the book on her desk, it says: *Magic is the tuning of needed energy for natural change.*

Her amber eyes move back and forth in front of the poem. Just above the orange neckline of her dress, above her right collarbone, she has tattooed three tiny black stars. She's sitting crosslegged in her swivel chair. Her feet are bare and dirty, with silver rings around each big toe.

"I know what this is," she says, and her hand comes up.

Before her fingers close around it, I fold the paper and tuck it into my back pocket.

Her hand still in the air, she points an index finger at me and says, "I've heard of those. It's a culling spell, right?"

Highlighted in the book on her desk, it says: *The ultimate product of death is invoking rebirth.*

Across the polished cherry top of the desk is a long deep gouge. I ask, what can she tell me about culling spells?

"All the literature mentions them," she says, and shrugs, "but they're supposed to be lost." She holds her hand out palm-up and says, "Let me see again."

And I say, how do they work?

And she wiggles her fingers.

And I shake my head no. I ask, how come it kills other people, but not the person who says it?

And tilting her head to one side a little, Mona says, "Why doesn't a gun kill the person who pulls the trigger? It's the same principle." She lifts both arms above her head and stretches, twisting her hands toward the ceiling. She says, "This doesn't work like a recipe in a cookbook. You can't dissect this with some electron microscope."

Her dress is sleeveless, and the hair under her arms is just regular mousy brown.

So, I say, how can it work on somebody who doesn't even hear the spell? I look at the radio. How can a spell work if you don't even say it out loud?

Mona Sabbat sighs. She turns her open book facedown on the desk and sticks the yellow highlighter behind one ear. She pulls open a desk drawer and takes out a pad and pencil, saying, "You don't have a clue, do you?"

Writing on the pad, she says, "When I was Catholic, this is years ago, I could say a seven-second Hail Mary. I could say a nine-second Our Father. When you get as much penance as I did, you get fast." She says, "When you get that fast, it's not even words anymore, but it's still a prayer."

She says, "All a spell does is focus an intention." She says this slow, word by word, and waits a beat. Her eyes on mine, she says, "If the practitioner's intention is strong enough, the object of the spell will fall asleep, no matter where."

The more emotion a person has bottled up, she says, the more powerful the spell. Mona Sabbat squints at me and says, "When was the last time you got laid?"

Almost two decades ago, but I do not tell her that.

"My guess," she says, "is you're a powder keg of something. Rage. Sorrow. Something." She stops writing, and flips through her highlighted book. Stopping at a page, she reads for a moment, then she flips to another page. "A well-balanced person," she says, "a functioning person, would have to read the song out loud to make someone fall asleep."

Still reading, she frowns and says, "Until you deal with your real personal issues, you'll never be able to control yourself."

I ask if her book says all that.

"Most of it's from Dr. Sara," she says.

And I say how the culling song does more than put people to sleep.

"How do you mean?" she says.

I mean they die. I say, are you sure you've never seen Helen Boyle with a book called *Poems and Rhymes from Around the World?*

Mona Sabbat's open hand drops to the desk and picks up her lunch wrapped in foil. She takes a bite, staring at the clock radio. She says, "Just now, on the radio," Mona says, "did you just do that?"

I nod.

"You just forced Dr. Sara to reincarnate?" she says.

I ask if she can just call Helen Hoover Boyle on her cell phone, and maybe I could talk to her.

My pager starts beeping.

And this Mona person says, "So you're saying Helen uses this same culling song?"

The message on my pager says to call Nash. The pager says it's important.

And I say, it's nothing I can prove, but Mrs. Boyle knows how. I say, I need her help so I can control it. So I can control myself.

And Mona Sabbat stops writing on the pad and tears off the page. She holds it halfway between us and says, "If you're serious about learning how to control this power, you need to come to a Wiccan practitioners' ritual." She shakes the paper at me and says, "We have over a thousand years of experience in one room." And she turns on the police scanner.

I take the paper. It's an address, date, and time.

The police scanner says, "Unit Bravo-nine, please respond to a code nine-fourteen at the Loomis Place Apartments, unit 5D."

"The mystical depth of this knowledge takes a lifetime to learn," she says. She picks up her lunch and peels back the foil. "Oh," she says, "and bring your favorite meat-free hot dish."

And the police scanner says, "Copy?"

Chapter 15

Helen Hoover Boyle takes her cell phone out of the green and white purse hanging from the crook of her elbow. She takes out a business card and looks from the card to the phone as she punches in a number, the little green buttons bright in the dim light. Bright green against the pink of her fingernail. The business card has a gold edge.

She presses the phone deep into the side of her pink hair. Into the phone, she says, "Yes, I'm somewhere in your lovely store, and I'm afraid I'll need some help finding my way out."

She leans into the note card taped to an armoire twice her height. Into the phone, she says, "I'm facing . . . ," and she reads, "an Adam-style neoclassical armoire with fire-gilded bronze arabesque cartouches."

She looks at me and rolls her eyes. Into the phone, she says, "It's marked seventeen thousand dollars."

Her feet step out of green high heels, and she stands flat-footed on the concrete floor in sheer white stockings. It's not the white that makes you think of underwear. It's more the white of the skin underneath. The stockings make her toes look webbed.

The suit she's wearing, the skirt is fitted to her hips. It's green, but not the green of a lime, more the green of a key lime pie. It's not the green of an avocado, but more the green of avocado bisque topped with a paper-thin sliver of lemon, served ice cold in a yellow Sèvres soup plate.

It's green the way a pool table with green felt looks under the yellow 1 ball, not the way it looks under the red 3.

I ask Helen Hoover Boyle what a code nine-fourteen is.

And she says, "A dead body."

And I say, I thought so.

Into the phone, she says, "Now, was that a left or right turn at the rosewood Hepplewhite dresser carved with anthemion details and flocked with powdered silk?"

She puts her hand over the phone and leans closer to me, saying, "You don't know Mona." She says, "I doubt if her little witch party means anything more than a mob of hippies dancing naked around a flat rock."

This close, her hair isn't a solid color of pink. Each curl is lighter pink along the outside edge, with blush, peach, rose, almost red, as you look deeper inside.

Into the phone, she says, "And if I pass the Cromwellian satin-wood lolling chair with ivory escutcheons, then I've gone too far. Got it."

To me, she says, "Lord, I wish you'd never told Mona. Mona will tell her boyfriend, and now I'll never hear the end of it."

The labyrinth of furniture crowds around us, all browns, reds, and black. Gilt and mirrors here and there.

With one hand, she fingers the diamond solitaire on her other hand. The diamond chunky and sharp. She twists it around so the diamond rises over her palm, and she presses her open palm on the face of the armoire and gouges an arrow pointing left.

Blazing a trail through history.

Into the phone, she says, "Thank you so much." She flips it shut and snaps it inside her purse.

The beads around her neck are some green stone, alternating with beads made of gold. Under these are strands of pearls. None of this jewelry I've ever seen before.

She steps back into her shoes and says, "From now on, I can see my job is going to be keeping you and Mona apart."

She fluffs the pink hair over her ear and says, "Follow me."

With her flat open hand, she gouges an arrow across the top of a table. A limned-oak Sheraton gateleg card table with a brass filigree railing, it says on the note card.

A cripple now.

Leading the way, Helen Hoover Boyle says, "I wish you'd let this whole issue drop." She says, "It really is no concern of yours."

Because I'm just a reporter, is what she means. Because I'm a reporter tracking down a story he can't ever risk telling the world. Because at best, this makes me a voyeur. At worst, a vulture.

She stops in front of a huge wardrobe with mirrored doors, and from behind her I can see myself reflected just over her shoulder. She snaps open her purse and takes out a small gold tube. "That's exactly what I mean," she says.

The note card says it's French Egyptian Revival with panels of papier-mâché palmette detailing and festooned with polychromed strapwork.

In the mirror, she twists the gold tube until a pink lipstick grows out.

And behind her, I say, what if I'm not just my job?

Maybe I'm not just some two-dimensional predator taking advantage of an interesting situation.

For whatever reason, Nash comes to mind.

I say, maybe I noticed the book in the first place because I used to have a copy. Maybe I used to have a wife and a daughter. What if I read the damn poem to my own family one night with the intention of putting them to sleep? Hypothetically speaking, of course, what if I killed them? I say. Is that the kind of credentials she's looking for?

She stretches her lips up and down and touches the lipstick to the pink lipstick already there.

I limp a step closer, asking, does that make me wounded enough in her book?

Her shoulders squared straight across, she rolls her lips together. They come apart slow, stuck together for the last moment.

God forbid anybody should ever suffer more than Helen Hoover Boyle.

And I say, maybe I've lost every bit as much as her.

And she twists her lipstick down. She snaps her lipstick in her purse and turns to face me.

Standing there, glittering and still, she says, "Hypothetically speaking?"

And I pull my face into a smile and say, of course.

With her open hand against the armoire, she gouges an arrow pointing right, and she starts walking, but slow, dragging her hand along the wall of cupboards and dressers, everything waxed and polished, ruining everything she touches.

Leading me on, she says, "Do you ever wonder where that poem originated?"

Africa, I say, staying right behind her.

"But the book it came from," she says. Walking, past gun cabinets and press cupboards and farthingale chairs, she says, "Witches call their collection of spells their Book of Shadows."

Poems and Rhymes from Around the World was published twenty years ago, I tell her. I did some calling around. The book had a pressrun of five hundred copies. The publisher, KinderHaus

Press, has since gone bankrupt, and the press plates and reprint rights belong to someone who bought them from the original author's estate. The author died of no apparent cause about three years ago. If that makes the book public domain, I don't know. I couldn't find out who now owns the rights.

And Helen Hoover Boyle stops dragging her diamond, midway across the face of a wide, beveled mirror, and says, "I own the rights. And I know where you're going with this. I bought the rights three years ago. Book dealers have managed to find about three hundred of those original five hundred books, and I've burned every one."

She says, "But that's not what's important."

I agree. What's important is finding the last few books, and containing this disaster. Doing damage control. What's important is learning a way to forget it ourselves. Maybe that's what Mona Sabbat and her group can teach us.

"Please," Helen says, "you're not still planning to go to her witch party?" She says, "What did you find out about the original author of the book?"

His name was Basil Frankie, and there was nothing original about him. He found out-of-print, public domain stories and combined them to create anthologies. Old medieval sonnets, bawdy limericks, nursery rhymes. Some of it he ripped out of old books he found. Some of it he lifted off the Internet. He wasn't very choosy. Anything he could get for free he'd lump into a book.

"But the source of this particular poem?" she says.

I don't know. It's probably some old book still packed in a box in the basement of a house somewhere.

"Not Frankie's house," says Helen Hoover Boyle. "I bought the whole estate. The kitchen trash was still under his sink, his underwear still folded in his dresser drawers, everything. It wasn't there."

And I have to ask, did she also kill him?

"Hypothetically speaking," she says, "if I had just killed my husband, after killing my son, wouldn't I be a little angry that some plagiarizing, lazy, irresponsible, greedy fool had planted the bomb that would destroy everyone I loved?"

Just like she hypothetically killed the Stuarts.

She says, "My point is that original Book of Shadows is still out there somewhere."

I agree. And we need to find it and destroy it.

And Helen Hoover Boyle smiles her pink smile. She says, "You must be kidding." She says, "Having the power of life and death isn't enough. You must wonder what other poems are in that book."

Hitting me as fast as a hiccup, me resting my weight on my good foot, just staring at her, I say no.

She says, "Maybe you can live forever."

And I say no.

And she says, "Maybe you can make anyone love you."

No.

And she says, "Maybe you can turn straw into gold."

And I say no and turn on my heel.

"Maybe you could bring about world peace," she says.

And I say no and start off between the walls of armoires and bookcases. Between the barricades of curio cabinets and head-boards, I head down another canyon of furniture.

Behind me, she calls, "Maybe you could turn sand into bread."

And I keep limping along.

And she calls, "Where are you going? This is the way out."

At an Irish pine vitrine with a broken pediment tympanum, I turn right. At a Chippendale bureau cabinet japanned in black lacquer, I turn left.

Her voice behind everything says, "Maybe you could cure the sick. Maybe you could heal the crippled."

At a Belgian sideboard with a cornice of egg and dart molding,

I turn right then left at an Edwardian standing specimen case with a Bohemian art-glass mural.

And the voice coming after me says, "Maybe you could clean the environment and turn the world into a paradise."

An arrow gouged in a piecrust occasional table points one way so I go the other.

And the voice says, maybe you could generate unlimited clean energy.

Maybe you could travel through time to prevent tragedy. To learn. To meet people.

Maybe you could give people rich full happy lives.

Maybe limping around a noisy apartment for the rest of your life isn't enough.

On a folding screen of blackwork embroidery, an arrow points one way, and I turn the other.

My pager goes off again, and it's Nash.

And the voice says, if you can kill someone, maybe you can bring them back.

Maybe this is my second chance.

The voice says, maybe you don't go to hell for the things you do. Maybe you go to hell for the things you don't do. The things you don't finish.

My pager goes off again, and it says the message is important.

And I keep on limping along.

Chapter 16

N ash isn't standing at the bar. He's sitting alone at a little table in the back, in the dark except for a little candle on the table, and I tell him, hey, I got his ten thousand calls on my pager. I ask, what's so important?

On the table is a newspaper, folded, with the headline saying:

Seven Dead in Mystery Plague

The subhead says:

Esteemed Local Editor and Public Leader
Believed to Be First Victim

Whom they mean, I have to read. It's Duncan, and it turns out his first name was Leslie. It's anybody's guess where they got the *esteemed* part. And the *leader* part.

So much for the journalist and the news being mutually exclusive.

Nash taps the newspaper with his finger and says, "You see this?"

And I tell him I've been out of the office all afternoon. And damn it. I forgot to file my next installment on crib death. Reading the front page, I see myself quoted. Duncan was more than just my editor, I'm saying, more than just my mentor. Leslie Duncan was like a father to me. Damn Oliphant and his sweaty hands.

Hitting me as fast as a chill, chilling me all down my back, the culling song spins through my head, and the body count grows. Somewhere, Oliphant must be sliding to the floor or toppling out of his chair. All my powder keg rage issues, they strike again.

The more people die, the more things stay the same.

An empty paper plate sits in front of Nash with just some waxed paper and yellow smears of potato salad on it, and Nash is twisting a paper napkin between his hands, twisting it into a long, thick cord, and, looking at me across the candle from him, he says, "We picked up the guy in your apartment building this afternoon." He says, "Between the guy's cats and the cockroaches, there's not much to autopsy."

The guy we saw fall down in here this morning, the sideburns guy with the cell phone, Nash says the medical examiner's stumped. Plus after that, three people dropped dead between here and the newspaper building.

"Then they found another one in the newspaper building," he says. "Died waiting for an elevator."

He says the medical examiner thinks these folks could all be dead of the same cause. They're saying plague, Nash says.

"But the police are really thinking drugs," he says. "Probably succinylcholine, either self-administered or somebody gave them an injection. It's a neuromuscular blocking agent. It relaxes you so much you quit breathing and die of anoxia."

The woman, the one behind the barricade at the movie shoot who came running with her arm out to stop me, the one with the walkie-talkie, the details of her were long black hair, a tight T-shirt over right-up tits. She had a decent little pooper in tight jeans. It could be she and Nash took the scenic route back to the hospital.

Another conquest.

Whatever Nash is so hot to tell me, I don't want to know.

He says, "But I think the police are wrong."

Nash whips the rolled paper napkin through the candle flame, and the flame jumps, stuttering up a curl of black smoke. The flame goes back to normal, and Nash says, "In case you want to take care of me the same's you took care of those other people," he says, "you have to know I wrote a letter explaining all this, and I left it with a friend, saying what I know at this point."

And I smile and ask what he means. What does he know?

And Nash holds the tip of his twisted paper a little over the candle flame and says, "I know you thought your neighbor was dead. I know I saw a guy drop dead in this bar with you looking at him, and four more died when you walked past them on your way back to work."

The tip of the paper's getting brown, and Nash says, "Granted, it's not much, but it's more than the police have right now."

The tip puffs into flame, just a tiny flame, and Nash says, "Maybe you can fill the police in on the rest of it."

The flame's getting bigger. There's people enough here that somebody's going to notice. Nash sitting here, setting fires in a bar, people are going to call the police.

And I say he's deluded.

The little torch is getting bigger.

The bartender looks over at us, at Nash's little fuse burning shorter and shorter.

Nash just watches the fire in his hand growing out of control.

The heat of it on my lips, the smoke in my eyes.

The bartender yells, "Hey! Quit screwing around!"

And Nash moves the burning napkin toward the waxed paper and paper plate on the table.

And I grab his wrist, his uniform cuff smeared yellow with mustard, and his skin underneath loose and soft, and I tell him, okay. I say, just stop, okay?

I say he has to promise never to tell.

And with the fuse still burning between us, Nash says, "Sure." He says, "I promise."

Chapter 17

H elen walks up with a wineglass in her hand, just a glimpse of red in the bottom, the glass almost empty.

And Mona says, "Where'd you get that?"

"My drink?" Helen says. She's wearing a thick coat made of some fur in different shades of brown with white on each tip. It's open in the front with a powder-blue suit underneath. She sips the last of the wine and says, "I got it off the bar. Over there, next to the bowl of oranges and that little brass statue."

And Mona digs both hands into her own red and black dread-locks and squeezes the top of her head. She says, "That's the *altar*." She points to the empty glass and says, "You just drank my sacrifice to *The Goddess*."

Helen presses the empty glass into Mona's hand and says,

"Well, how about you get *The Goddess* another sacrifice, but make it a double this time."

We're in Mona's apartment, where all the furniture is pushed out onto a little patio behind sliding glass doors and covered with a blue plastic tarp. All that's left is the empty living room with a little room branching off one side where the dinette set should be. The walls and shag carpet are beige. The bowl of oranges and the brass statue of somebody Hindu, dancing, they're on the fireplace mantel with yellow daisies and pink carnations scattered around them. The light switches are taped over with masking tape so you can't use them. Instead, Mona's got some flat rocks on the floor with candles set on them, purple and white candles, some lit, some not. In the fireplace, instead of a fire, more candles are burning. Strands of white smoke drift up from little cones of brown incense set on the flat rocks with the candles.

The only real light is when Mona opens the refrigerator or the microwave oven.

Through the walls come horses screaming and cannon fire. Either a brave, stubborn southern belle is trying to keep the Union army from burning the apartment next door, or somebody's television is too loud.

Down through the ceiling comes a fire siren and people screaming that we're supposed to ignore. Then gunshots and tires squealing, sounds we have to pretend are okay. They don't mean anything. It's just television. An explosion vibrates down from the upstairs. A woman begs someone not to rape her. It's not real. It's just a movie. We're the culture that cried wolf.

These drama-holics. These peace-ophobics.

With her black fingernails, Mona takes the empty wineglass, the lip smeared with Helen's pink lipstick, and she walks away barefoot, wearing a white terry-cloth bathrobe into the kitchen.

The doorbell rings.

Mona crosses back through the living room. Putting another

glass of red wine on the mantel, she says, "Do not embarrass me in front of my coven," and she opens the door.

On the doorstep is a short woman wearing glasses with thick frames of black plastic. The woman's wearing oven mitts and holding a covered casserole dish in front of her.

I brought a deli take-out box of three-bean salad. Helen brought pasta from Chez Chef.

The glasses woman scrapes her clogs on the doormat. She looks at Helen and me and says, "Mulberry, you have guests."

And Mona conks herself in the temple with the heel of her hand and says, "That's me she means. That's my Wiccan name, I mean. Mulberry." She says, "Sparrow, this is Mr. Streator."

And Sparrow nods.

And Mona says, "And this is my boss——"

"Chinchilla," Helen says.

The microwave oven starts beeping, and Mona leads Sparrow into the kitchen. Helen goes to the mantel and takes a drink from the glass of wine.

The doorbell rings. And Mona calls from the kitchen for us to answer it.

This time, it's a kid with long blond hair and a red goatee, wearing gray sweatpants and a sweatshirt. He's carrying a Crock-Pot with a brown-glass lid. Something sticky and brown has boiled up around the lip, and the underside of the glass lid is fogged with condensation. He steps inside the door and hands the Crock-Pot to me. He kicks off tennis shoes and pulls the sweatshirt off over his head, his hair flying everywhere. He lays the shirt on top of the Crock-Pot in my hands and lifts his leg to pull first one leg then the other leg out of his sweatpants. He puts the pants in my arms, and he's standing here, hands on his hips, dick-and-balls naked.

Helen pulls the front of her coat shut and throws back the last of the wine.

The Crock-Pot is heavy and hot with the smell of brown sugar and either tofu or the dirty gray sweatpants.

And Mona says, "Oyster!" and she's standing beside us. She takes the clothes and the Crock-Pot from me, saying, "Oyster, this is Mr. Streator." She says, "Everybody, this is my boyfriend, Oyster."

And the kid shakes the hair off his eyes and looks at me. He says, "Mulberry thinks you have a culling poem." His dick tapers to a dribbling pink stalactite of wrinkled foreskin. A silver ring pierces the tip.

And Helen gives me a look, smiling but with her teeth clenched.

This kid, Oyster, grabs the terry-cloth lapels of Mona's bathrobe and says, "Jeez, you have a lot of clothes on." He leans into her and kisses her over the Crock-Pot.

"We do ritual nudity," Mona says, looking at the floor. She blushes and motions with the Crock-Pot, saying, "Oyster? This is Mrs. Boyle, who I work for."

The details about Oyster are his hair, it looks shattered, the way a pine tree looks struck by lightning, splintered blond and standing up in every direction. He's got one of those young bodies. The arms and legs look segmented, big with muscles, then narrow at the joints, the knees and elbows and waist.

Helen holds out her hand, and Oyster takes it, saying, "A peridot ring . . ."

Standing there naked and young, he lifts Helen's hand all the way to his face. Standing there all tan and muscled, he looks from her ring, down the length of her arm, to her eyes and says, "A stone this passionate would overpower most people." And he kisses it.

"We do ritual nudity," Mona says, "but you don't have to. I mean you *really* don't have to." She nods toward the kitchen and says, "Oyster, come help me for a little."

And going, Oyster looks at me and says, "Clothing is dishonesty in its purest form." He smiles with just half his mouth, winks, and says, "Nice tie, Dad."

And I'm counting 1, counting 2, counting 3 . . .

After Mona's gone into the kitchen, Helen turns to me and says, "I can't believe you told another person."

She means Nash.

It wasn't as if I had a choice. Besides, no copies of the poem are available. I told him I burned mine, and I've burned every copy I found in print. He doesn't know about Helen Hoover Boyle or Mona Sabbat. There's no way he can use the information.

Okay, so there are still a few dozen copies in public libraries. Maybe we can track them down and eliminate page 27 while we hunt for the original source material.

"The Book of Shadows," Helen says.

The grimoire, as witches call it. The book of spells. All the power in the world.

The doorbell rings, and the next man drops his baggy shorts and peels off his T-shirt and tells us his name is Hedgehog. The details about Hedgehog include the empty skin shaking on his arms and chest and ass. His curly black pubic hair matches the couple of hairs stuck to my palm after we shake hands.

Helen's hands draw up inside the cuffs of her coat sleeves, and she goes to the mantel, takes an orange from the altar, and starts to peel it.

A man named Badger with a real parrot on one shoulder arrives. A woman named Clematis arrives. A Lobelia arrives. A Bluebird rings the doorbell. Then a Possum. Then someone named Lentils arrives, or someone brings lentils, it's not clear which. Helen drinks another sacrifice. Mona comes out of the kitchen with Oyster, but without her bathrobe.

What's left is a pile of dirty clothes inside the front door, and Helen and I are the only ones still dressed. Deep in the pile a phone rings, and Sparrow digs it out. Wearing just her black-framed glasses, her breasts hanging as she leans over the pile, Sparrow answers the phone, "Dormer, Dingus and Diggs, Attorneys-at-Law . . ." She says, "Describe the rash, please."

It takes a minute to recognize Mona from just her head and the pile of chains around her neck. You don't want to get caught looking anywhere else, but her pubic hair is shaved. From straight on, her thighs are two perfect parentheses with her shaved V between them. From the side, her breasts seem to reach out, trying to touch people with her pink nipples. From behind, the small of her back splits into her two solid buttocks, and I'm counting 4, counting 5, counting 6 . . .

Oyster's carrying a white deli take-out carton.

A woman named Honeysuckle in just a calico head wrap talks about her past lives.

And Helen says, "Doesn't reincarnation strike you as just another form of procrastination?"

I ask, when do we eat?

And Mona says, "Jeez, you sound just like my father."

I ask Helen how she keeps from killing everybody here.

And she takes another glass of wine off the mantel, saying, "Anybody in this room, and it would be a mercy killing." She drinks half and gives the rest to me.

The incense smells like jasmine, and everything in the room smells like the incense.

Oyster steps to the center of the room and holds the deli carton over his head and says, "Okay, who brought this abortion?"

It's my three-bean salad.

And Mona says, "Please, Oyster, don't."

And holding the deli carton by its little wire handle, the handle pinched between just two fingers, Oyster says, " 'Meat-free' means no meat. Now fess up. Who brought this?" The hair under his raised arm is bright orange. So is his other body hair, down below.

I say, it's just bean salad.

"With?" Oyster says, and jiggles the carton.

With nothing.

The room's so quiet you can hear the Battle of Gettysburg next door. You can hear the folk song guitar of somebody depressed in the apartment upstairs. An actor screams and a lion roars and bombs whistle down from the sky.

"With Worcestershire sauce in the dressing," Oyster says. "That means anchovies. That means meat. That means cruelty and death." He holds the carton in one hand and points at it with his other, saying, "This is going down the toilet where it belongs."

And I'm counting 7, counting 8 . . .

Sparrow is giving everyone small round stones out of a basket she carries in one hand. She gives one to me. It's gray and cold, and she says, "Hold on to this, and tune to the vibration of its energy. This will put us all on the same vibration for the ritual."

You hear the toilet flush.

The parrot on Badger's shoulder keeps twisting its head around and yanking out green feathers with its beak. Then the bird tilts its head back and gulps each feather in jerking, whiplash bites. Where the feathers are gone, plucked, the skin looks dimpled and raw. The man, Badger, has a folded towel thrown over his shoulder for the parrot to grip, and the towel is spotted down the back with yellowy bird shit. The bird yanks another feather and eats it.

Sparrow gives a stone to Helen, and she snaps it into her powder-blue handbag.

I take the wineglass from her and sip it. In the newspaper today, it says how the man at the elevator, the man I wished to death, he had three children, all under six years old. The cop I killed was supporting his elderly parents so they wouldn't be placed in a nursing home. He and his wife were foster parents. He coached Little League and soccer. The woman with the walkie-talkie, she was two weeks pregnant.

I drink more of the wine. It tastes like pink lipstick.

In the newspaper today is an ad that says:

Attention Owners of Dorsett Fine China

The ad copy says: "If you feel nauseated or lose bowel control after eating, please call the following number."

To me, Oyster says, "Mulberry thinks you killed Dr. Sara, but I don't think you know jack shit."

Mona reaches up to put another sacrifice on the mantel and Helen lifts the glass out of her fingers.

To me, Oyster says, "The only power of life and death you have is every time you order a hamburger at McDonald's." His face stuck in my face, he says, "You just pay your filthy money, and somewhere else, the ax falls."

And I'm counting 9, counting 10 . . .

Sparrow shows me a thick manual open in her hands. Inside are pictures of wands and iron pots. There are pictures of bells and quartz crystals, different colors and sizes of everything. There are black-handled knives, called *athame*. Sparrow says this so it rhymes with "whammy." She shows me photos of herbs, bundled so you can use them to sprinkle purification water. She shows me amulets, polished to deflect negative energy. A white-handled ritual knife is called a *bolline*.

Her breasts rest on the open catalog, covering half of each page.

Standing next to me, the muscles jumping in his neck, making fists with both hands, Oyster says, "Do you know why most survivors of the Holocaust are vegan? It's because they know what it's like to be treated like an animal."

The body heat coming off him, he says, "In egg production, did you know all the male chicks are ground up alive and spread as fertilizer?"

Sparrow flips through her catalog and points at something, saying, "If you check around, you'll find we offer the best deals for ritual tools in the medium price range."

The next sacrifice to *The Goddess*, I drink.

The one after that, Helen downs.

Oyster circles the room. He comes back to say, "Did you know that most pigs don't bleed to death in the few seconds before they're drowned in scalding, hundred-and-forty-degree water?"

The sacrifice after that, I get. The wine tastes like jasmine incense. The wine tastes like animal blood.

Helen takes the empty wineglass into the kitchen, and there's a flash of real light as she opens the refrigerator and takes out a jug of red wine.

And Oyster sticks his chin over my shoulder from behind and says, "Most cows don't die right away." He says, "They put a snare around the cow's neck and drag it screaming through the slaughterhouse, cutting off the front and back legs while it's still alive."

Behind him is a naked girl named Starfish, who flips open a cell phone and says, "Dooley, Donner and Dunne, Attorneys-at-Law." She says, "Tell me, what color is your fungus?"

Badger comes out of the bathroom, ducking to get his parrot through the doorway, a shred of paper stuck in his butt crack. Naked, his skin looks dimpled and raw. Plucked. If the bird sits on his shoulder while he sits on the toilet, I don't want to know.

And across the room is Mona.

Mulberry.

She's laughing with Honeysuckle. She's pinned her red and black dreadlocks up into a pile with just her little face sticking out the bottom. On her fingers are rings with heavy red-glass jewels. Around her neck, the carpet of silver chains comes down to a pile of amulets and pendants and charms on her breasts. Costume jewelry. A little girl playing dress-up. Barefoot.

She's the age my daughter would be, if I still had a daughter.

Helen stumbles back into the room. She pinches her tongue between two fingers and then goes around the room, using the two wet fingers to pinch out the cones of incense. She leans back against the fireplace mantel and lifts the glass of wine to her pink mouth. Over the glass, she watches the room. She watches Oyster circling me.

He's the age her son, Patrick, would be.

Helen's the age my wife would be, if I had a wife.

Oyster's the son she would have, if she had a son.

Hypothetically speaking, of course.

This might be the life I had, if I had a life. My wife distant and drunk. My daughter exploring some crackpot cult. Embarrassed by us, her parents. Her boyfriend would be this hippie asshole, trying to pick a fight with me, her dad.

And maybe you can go back in time.

Maybe you can raise the dead. All the dead, past and present.

Maybe this is my second chance. This is exactly the way my life might have turned out.

Helen in her chinchilla coat is watching the parrot eat itself. She's watching Oyster.

And Mona's shouting, "Everybody. Everybody." She's saying, "It's time to start the Invocation. So if we could just create the sacred space, we can get started."

Next door, the Civil War veterans are limping home to sad music and Reconstruction.

With Oyster circling me, the rock in my fist is warm by now. And I'm counting 11, counting 12 . . .

Mona Sabbat has got to come with us. Someone without blood on her hands. Mona and Helen and me, and Oyster, the four of us will hit the road together. Just another dysfunctional family. A family vacation. The quest for an unholy grail.

With a hundred paper tigers to slay along the way. A hundred libraries to plunder. Books to disarm. The whole world to save from culling.

Lobelia says to Grenadine, "Did you read about those dead people in the paper? They say it's like Legionnaires' disease, but it looks like black magic, if you ask me."

And with her arms spread, the plain brown hair under her

arms showing, Mona is herding people into the center of the room.

Sparrow points at something in her catalog and says, "This is the minimum you'll need to get started."

Oyster shakes the hair off his eyes and sticks his chin at me. He comes around to poke his index finger into my chest, poking it there, hard, pinned in the middle of my blue tie, and he says, "Listen, Dad." Poking me, he says, "The only culling song you know is 'Make mine medium-well done.' "

And I stop counting.

Fast as a muscle twitch, muscling Oyster back, I shove hard and slap the kid away, my hands loud against the kid's bare skin, everybody quiet and watching, and the culling song echoes through my head.

And I've killed again. Mona's boyfriend. Helen's son. Oyster stands there another moment, looking at me, the hair hanging over his eyes.

And the parrot falls off Badger's shoulder.

Oyster puts his hands up, fingers spread, and says, "Chill out, Dad," and goes with Sparrow and everybody to look at the parrot, dead, at Badger's feet. Dead and plucked half naked. And Badger prods the bird with his sandal and says, "Plucky?"

I look at Helen.

My wife. In this new creepy way. Till death do us part.

And maybe, if you can kill someone, maybe you can bring them back.

And Helen's already looking at me, the smeared-pink glass in her hand. She shakes her face at me and says, "I didn't do it." She holds up three fingers, her thumb and pinkie touching in front, and says, "Witch's honor. I swear."

Chapter 18

Here and now, me writing this, I'm near Biggs Junction, Oregon. Parked alongside Interstate 84, the Sarge and me have an old fur coat heaped on the shoulder of the road next to our car. The fur coat, spattered with ketchup, circled by flies, it's our bait.

This week, there's another miracle in the tabloids.

It's something folks call the Roadkill Jesus Christ. The tabloids call him "The I-84 Messiah." Some guy who stops along the highway, wherever there's a dead animal, he lays his hands on it, and Amen. The ragged cat or crushed dog, even a deer folded in half by a tractor-trailer, they gasp and sniff the air. They stand on their broken legs and blink their bird-pecked eyes.

Folks have this on video. They have snapshots posted on the Internet.

The cat or porcupine or coyote, it'll stand there another minute, the Roadkill Christ cradling its head in his arms, whispering to it.

Two minutes after it was shredded fur and bones, a meal for magpies and crows, the deer or dog or raccoon will run away complete, restored, perfect.

The Sarge and me, a ways down the highway from us, an old man pulls his pickup truck off the road. He gets out of the cab and lifts a plaid blanket out of the bed of the truck. He squats to lay the blanket on the side of the road, traffic blasting past him in the hot morning air.

The old man picks at the edges of the plaid blanket to uncover a dead dog. A wrinkled heap of brown fur, not too much different than my heap of fur coat.

The Sarge snaps the clip out of his pistol, and it's full of bullets. He snaps the clip back home.

The old man leans down, both his hands flat open on the hot asphalt, cars and trucks blasting past in both directions, and he rubs his cheek against the pile of brown fur.

He stands and looks up and down the highway. He gets back into the cab of his pickup and lights a cigarette. He waits.

The Sarge and I, we wait.

Here we are, a week late. Always one step behind. After the fact.

The first sighting of the Roadkill Christ, it was a crew of state workers shoveling up a dead dog a few miles from here. Before they could get it bagged, a rental car pulled over on the highway shoulder behind them. It was a man and a woman, the man driving. The woman stayed in the car, and the man jumped out and ran up to the road crew. He shouted for them to wait. He said he could help.

The dog was just maggots and bones inside a scrap of fur.

The man was young, blond, with his long blond hair whipping in the wind from cars blasting past them. He had a red goatee and scars cut sideways across both cheeks, just under his eyes. The scars were dark red, and the young man reached into the garbage bag with the dead dog and told the crew—it wasn't dead.

And the road crew laughed. They threw their shovel into their truck.

And something inside the garbage bag whimpered.

It barked.

Now, here and now, while I write this, while the old man waits down the road from us, smoking. The traffic blasting past. On the other side of Interstate 84, a family in a station wagon opens a quilt on the gravel shoulder of the road, and inside is a dead orange cat. A ways from them, a woman and a child sit in lawn chairs next to a hamster on a paper towel.

A ways from them, an older couple stands holding an umbrella to shade a young woman, the young woman bony and twisted sideways in a wheelchair.

The old man, the mother and child, the family and older couple, their eyes scan every car as it goes past.

The Roadkill Christ appears in a different car every time, a two-door or a four-door or a pickup, sometimes on a motorcycle. Once in a motor home.

In the snapshots people take, in the videos, it's always the flying blond hair, the red goatee, the scars. It's always the same man. The outline of a woman waits in the distance in a car, truck, whatever.

While I'm writing this, the Sarge sights down the barrel of his pistol at our pile of fur coat. The ketchup and flies. Our bait. And like everyone else here, we're waiting for a miracle. For a messiah.

Chapter 19

Everywhere outside the car it was yellow. Yellow to the horizon. Not a lemon yellow, more a tennis-ball yellow. It was the way the ball looks on a bright green tennis court. The world on both sides of the highway, all this one color.

Yellow.

Billowing, foaming big waves of yellow move in the hot wind from the cars going past, spreading from the highway's gravel shoulder to the yellow hills. Yellow. Throwing yellow light into our car. Helen, Mona, Oyster, me, all of us. Our skin and eyes. The details of the whole world. Yellow.

"Brassica tournefortii," Oyster says, "Moroccan mustard in full bloom."

We're in the leather smell of Helen's big Realtor car with her driving. Helen and I sit up front, Oyster and Mona in the back. On the seat between Helen and me is her daily planner book, the red leather binding sticking to the brown leather seat. There's an atlas of the United States. There's a computer printout of cities with libraries that have the poems book. There's Helen's little blue purse, looking green in the yellow light.

"What I'd give to be a Native American," Mona says, and leans her forehead against the window, "to just be a free Blackfoot or Sioux two hundred years ago, you know, just living in harmony with all that natural beauty."

To see what Mona's feeling, I put my forehead against my window. Against the air-conditioning, the glass is blazing hot.

Creepy coincidence, but the atlas shows the entire state of California colored this same bright yellow.

And Oyster blows out his nose, one quick snort that rocks his head back. He shakes his face at Mona and says, "No Indian ever lived with *that*."

The cowboys didn't have tumbleweeds, he says. It wasn't until the late nineteenth century that tumbleweed seeds, Russian thistles, came over from Eurasia in the wool of sheep. Moroccan mustard came over in the dirt that sailing ships used for ballast. The silver trees out there, those are Russian olives, *Elaeagnus augustifolia.* The hundreds of white fuzzy rabbit ears growing along the highway shoulder are *Verbascum thapsus,* woolly mulleins. The twisted dark trees we just passed, *Robinia pseudoacacia,* black locust. The dark green brush flowering bright yellow is Scotch broom, *Cytisus scoparius.*

They're all part of a biological pandemic, he says.

"Those old Hollywood westerns," Oyster says, looking out the window at Nevada next to the highway, he says, "with the tumbleweeds and cheatgrass and shit?" He shakes his head and says, "None of this is native, but it's all we have left." He says, "Almost nothing in nature is natural anymore."

Oyster kicks the back of the front seat and says, "Hey, Dad. What's the big daily newspaper in Nevada?"

Reno or Vegas? I say.

And looking out the window, the reflected light making his eyes yellow, Oyster says, "Both. Carson City, too. All of them."

And I tell him.

The forests along the West Coast are choked with Scotch broom and French broom and English ivy and Himalayan blackberries, he says. The native trees are dying from the gypsy moths imported in 1860 by Leopold Trouvelot, who wanted to breed them for silk. The deserts and prairies are choked with mustard and cheatgrass and European beach grass.

Oyster fingers open the buttons on his shirt, and inside, against the skin of his chest, is a beaded something. It's the size of a wallet, hanging around his neck from a beaded string. "Hopi medicine bag," he says. "Pretty spiritual, huh?"

Helen, looking at him in the rearview mirror, her hands on the steering wheel in skintight calfskin driving gloves, she says, "Nice abs."

Oyster shrugs his shirt off his shoulders and the beaded bag hangs between his nipples, his chest pumped up on each side of it. The skin's tanned and hairless down to his navel. The bag's covered solid with blue beads except for a cross of red beads in the center. His tan looks orange in the yellow light. His blond hair looks on fire.

"I made it," Mona says. "It took me since last February."

Mona with her dreadlocks and crystal necklaces. I ask if she's a Hopi Indian.

With his fingers, Oyster fishes around inside the bag.

And Helen says, "Mona, you're not a native *anything*. Your real last name is Steinner."

"You don't have to be Hopi," Mona says. "I made it from a pattern in a book."

"Then it's not really a Hopi anything," Helen says.

And Mona says, "It is. It looks just like the one in the book."
She says, "I'll show you."

From out of his little beaded bag, Oyster takes a cell phone.

"The fun part about primitive crafts is they're so easy to make while you watch TV," Mona says. "And they put you in touch with all sorts of ancient energies and stuff."

Oyster flips the phone open and pulls out the antenna. He punches in a number. A curve of dirt shows under his fingernail.

Helen watches him in the rearview mirror.

Mona leans forward over her knees and drags a canvas knapsack off the floor of the backseat. She takes out a tangle of cords and feathers. They look like chicken feathers, dyed bright Easter shades of pink and blue. Brass coins and beads made of black glass hang on the cords. "This is a Navajo dream catcher I'm making," she says. She shakes it, and some of the cords come untangled and hang loose. Some beads fall into the knapsack in her lap. Pink feathers float loose in the air, and she says, "I thought to make it more powerful by using some I Ching coins. To sort of superenergize it."

Somewhere under the knapsack, in her lap, the shaved V between her thighs. The glass beads roll there.

Into the phone, Oyster says, "Yeah, I need the number for the retail display advertising department at the *Carson City Telegraph-Star.*" A pink feather drifts near his face, and he blows it away.

With her black-painted fingernails, Mona picks at some of the knots, saying, "It's harder than the book makes it look."

Oyster's one hand holds the phone to his ear. His other hand rubs the beaded bag around his chest.

Mona pulls a book out of her canvas knapsack and passes it to me in the front seat.

Oyster sees Helen, still watching him in the rearview mirror, and he winks at her and tweaks his nipple.

For whatever reason, Oedipus Rex comes to mind.

Somewhere below his belt, the pointed pink stalactite of his foreskin, pierced with its little steel ring. How could Helen want that?

"Old-time ranchers planted cheatgrass because it would green up fast in the spring and provide early forage for grazing cattle," Oyster says, nodding his head at the world outside.

This first patch of cheatgrass was in southern British Columbia, Canada, in 1889. But fire spreads it. Every year, it dries to gunpowder, and now land that used to burn every ten years, it burns every year. And the cheatgrass recovers fast. Cheatgrass loves fire. But the native plants, the sagebrush and desert phlox, they don't. And every year it burns, there's more cheatgrass and less anything else. And the deer and antelope that depended on those other plants are gone now. So are the rabbits. So are the hawks and owls that ate the rabbits. The mice starve, so the snakes that ate the mice starve.

Today, cheatgrass dominates the inland deserts from Canada to Nevada, covering an area over twice the size of the state of Nebraska and spreading by thousands of acres per year.

The big irony is, even cattle hate cheatgrass, Oyster says. So the cows, they eat the rare native bunch grasses. What's left of them.

Mona's book is called *Traditional Tribal Hobby-Krafts*. When I open it, more pink and blue feathers drift out.

"Now, my new life's dream is I want to find a really straight tree, you know," Mona says, a pink feather caught in her dreadlocks, "and make a totem pole or something."

"When you think about it from a native plant perspective," Oyster says, "Johnny Appleseed was a fucking biological terrorist."

Johnny Appleseed, he says, might as well be handing out smallpox.

Oyster's punching another number on his cell phone. He kicks the back of the front seat and says, "Mom, Dad? What's a really posh restaurant in Reno, Nevada?"

And Helen shrugs and looks at me. She says, "The Desert Sky Supper Club in Tahoe is very nice."

Into his cell phone, Oyster says, "I'd like to place a three-column display ad." Looking out the window, he says, "It should be three columns by six inches deep, and the top line of copy should read, 'Attention Patrons of the Desert Sky Supper Club.'"

Oyster says, "The second line should say, 'Have you recently contracted a near-fatal case of campylobacter food poisoning? If so, please call the following number to be part of a class-action lawsuit.'"

Then Oyster gives a phone number. He fishes a credit card out of his medicine bag and reads the number and expiration date into the phone. He says for the account rep to call him after it's typeset and check the final ad copy over the phone. He says for the ad to run every day for the next week, in the restaurant section. He flips the phone shut and presses the antenna back inside.

"The way yellow fever and smallpox killed off your Native Americans," he says, "we brought Dutch elm disease to America in a shipment of logs for a veneer mill in 1930 and brought chestnut blight in 1904. Another pathogenic fungus is killing off the eastern beeches. The Asian long-horned beetle, introduced to New York in 1996, is expected to wipe out North American maples."

To control prairie dog populations, Oyster says, ranchers introduced bubonic plague to the prairie dog colonies, and by 1930, about 98 percent of the dogs were dead. The plague has spread to kill another thirty-four species of native rodents, and every year a few unlucky people.

For whatever reason, the culling song comes to mind.

"Me," Mona says as I pass her back the book, "I like the ancient traditions. My hope is this trip will be, you know, like my own personal vision quest. And I'll come up with an Indian name and be," she says, "transformed."

Out of his Hopi bag, Oyster takes a cigarette and says, "You mind?"

And I tell him yes.

And Helen says, "Not at all." And it's her car.

And I'm counting 1, counting 2, counting 3 . . .

What we think of as nature, Oyster says, everything's just more of us killing the world. Every dandelion's a ticking atom bomb. Biological pollution. Pretty yellow devastation.

The way you can go to Paris or Beijing, Oyster says, and everywhere there's a McDonald's hamburger, this is the ecological equivalent of franchised life-forms. Every place is the same place. Kudzu. Zebra mussels. Water hyacinths. Starlings. Burger Kings.

The local natives, anything unique gets squeezed out.

"The only biodiversity we're going to have left," he says, "is Coke versus Pepsi."

He says, "We're landscaping the whole world one stupid mistake at a time."

Just staring out his window, Oyster takes a plastic cigarette lighter out of the beaded medicine bag. He shakes the lighter, smacking it against the palm of one hand.

A pink feather from the book, I sniff it and imagine Mona's hair has this same smell. Twirling the feather between two fingers, I ask Oyster, on the phone just now—his call to the newspaper—what he's up to.

Oyster lights his cigarette. He tucks the plastic lighter and the cell phone back in his medicine bag.

"It's how he makes money," Mona says. She's picking apart the tangles and knots in her dream catcher. Between her arms, inside her orange blouse, her breasts reach out with their little pink nipples.

And I'm counting 4, counting 5, counting 6 . . .

Both his hands buttoning his shirt, his mouth pinched around the cigarette, and his eyes squinting against the smoke, Oyster says, "Remember Johnny Appleseed?"

Helen turns up the air-conditioning.

And buttoning his collar, Oyster says, "Don't worry, Dad. This is just me planting my seeds."

Looking out at all the yellow, with his yellow eyes, he says, "It's just my generation trying to destroy the existing culture by spreading our own contagion."

Chapter 20

The woman opens her front door, and here are Helen and I on her front porch, me carrying Helen's cosmetic case, standing a half-step behind her as Helen points the long pink nail of her index finger and says, "If you can give me fifteen minutes, I can give you a whole new you."

Helen's suit is red, but not a strawberry red. It's more the red of a strawberry mousse, topped with whipped crème fraîche and served in a stemmed crystal compote. Inside her pink cloud of hair, her earrings sparkle pink and red in the sunlight.

The woman's drying her hands in a kitchen towel. She's wearing men's brown moccasins with no socks. A bib apron patterned with little yellow chickens covers her whole front, and some kind of machine-washable dress underneath. With the back of one hand, she pushes some hair off her forehead. The yellow chickens are all holding kitchen tools, ladles and spoons, in their beaks. Looking at us through the rusted screen door, the woman says, "Yes?"

Helen looks back at me standing behind her. She looks back over her shoulder at Mona and Oyster ducked down, hiding in the car parked at the curb. Oyster whispering into his phone, "Is the itching constant or intermittent?"

Helen Hoover Boyle brings the fingertips of one hand together at her chest, the mess of pink gems and pearls hiding her silk blouse underneath. She says, "Mrs. Pelson? We're here from Miracle Makeover."

As she talks, Helen throws her closed hand open toward the woman, as if she's scattering the words.

Helen says, "My name is Mrs. Brenda Williams." With her pink fingertips, she scatters the words back over her shoulder, saying, "And this is my husband, Robert Williams." She says, "And we have a very special gift for you today."

The woman inside the screen door looks down at the cosmetic case in my hand.

And Helen says, "May we come in?"

It was supposed to be easier than this.

This whole traveling around, just dropping into libraries, taking a book off the shelf, sitting on a toilet in the library bathroom and cutting out the page. Then, flush. It was supposed to be that quick.

The first couple libraries, no problem. The next, the book isn't on the shelf. In library whispers, Mona and I go to the checkout desk and ask. Helen's waiting in the car with Oyster.

The librarian's a guy with his long straight hair pulled back in a ponytail. He's got earrings in both ears, pirate loop earrings, and he's wearing a plaid sweater vest and says the book is—he scrolls up and down his computer screen—the book is checked out.

"It's really important," Mona says. "I had it before that, and I left something between the pages."

Sorry, the guy says.

"Can you tell us who has it?" Mona says.

And the guy says, sorry. No can do.

And I'm counting 1, counting 2, counting 3 . . .

Sure, everybody wants to play God, but for me it's a full-time job.

I'm counting 4, counting 5 . . .

A beat later, Helen Hoover Boyle's standing at the checkout desk. She smiles until the librarian looks up from his computer, and she spreads her hands, her rings bright and crowded on each finger.

She smiles and says, "Young man? My daughter left an old family photograph between the pages of a certain book." She wiggles her fingers and says, "You can follow the rules, or you can do a good deed and take your pick."

The librarian watches her fingers, the prism colors and stars of broken light dancing across his face. He licks his lips. Then he shakes his head no and says it's just not worth it. The person with the book will complain and he'll get fired.

"We promise," Helen says, "we won't lose you your job."

In the car, I waiting with Mona, counting 27, counting 28, counting 29 . . . , trying the only way I know not to kill everybody in the library and look up the address on the computer myself.

Helen comes out to the car with a sheet of paper in her hand. She leans in the open driver's-side window and says, "Good news and bad news."

Mona and Oyster are lying across the backseat, and they sit up. I'm on the shotgun side of the front seat, counting.

And Mona says, "They have three copies, but they're all checked out."

And Helen gets in behind the steering wheel and says, "I know a million ways to cold-call."

And Oyster shakes the hair off his eyes and says, "Good job, Mom."

The first house went easy enough. And the second.

In the car between house calls, Helen picks through the gold tubes and shiny boxes, her lipstick and makeup, her cosmetic case open in her lap. She twists a pink lipstick up and squints at it, saying, "I'm never using any of this again. If I'm not mistaken, that last woman had ringworm."

Mona leans forward from the backseat, looking over Helen's shoulder, and says, "You're really good at this."

Screwing open little round boxes of eye shadow, looking and sniffing at their tan or pink or peach insides, Helen says, "I've had a lot of practice."

She looks at herself in the rearview mirror and pulls around a few strands of pink hair. She looks at her watch, pinching the face between a thumb and index finger, and she says, "I shouldn't tell you this, but this was my first real job."

By now we're parked outside a rusted trailer house sitting in a square of dead grass scattered with children's plastic toys. Helen snaps her case shut. She looks at me sitting beside her and says, "You ready to try it again?"

Inside the trailer, talking to the woman in the apron covered with little chickens, Helen's saying, "There's absolutely no cost or obligation on your part," and she backs the woman into the sofa.

Sitting across from the woman, the woman sitting so close their knees almost touch, Helen reaches toward her with a soft brush and says, "Suck in your cheeks, dear."

With one hand, she grabs a handful of the woman's hair and pulls it straight up into the air. The woman's hair is blond with an inch of brown at the roots. With her other hand, Helen runs a comb down the hair in fast strokes, holding the longer strands up, and crushing the shorter brown ones down against the scalp. She grabs another handful and rats, teases, back-combs until all but the longest hairs are crushed and tangled against the scalp. With the comb, she smooths the long blond strands over the ratted short hairs until the woman's head is a huge fluffed bubble of blond hair.

And I say, so *that's* how you do that.

It's identical to Helen's hairdo only blond.

On the coffee table in front of the sofa is a big arrangement of roses and lilies, but wilted and brown, the flowers standing in a green-glass vase from a florist, with only a little black water in the bottom. On the dinette table in the kitchen are more big flower arrangements, just dead stalks in thick, stinking water. Lined up on the floor, against the back wall of the living room are more vases, each holding a block of green foam pincushioned with curled, wasted roses or black, spindly carnations growing gray mold. Stuck in with each bouquet is a little card saying: *In Deepest Sympathy*.

And Helen says, "Now put your hands over your face," and she starts shaking a can of hair spray. She fogs the woman with hair spray.

The woman cowers blind, bent forward a little, with both hands pressed over her face.

And Helen jerks her head toward the rooms at the other end of the trailer.

And I go.

Pumping a mascara brush in its tube, she says, "You don't mind if my husband uses your bathroom, do you?" Helen says, "Now, look up at the ceiling, dear."

In the bathroom, there are dirty clothes separated into different-colored piles on the floor. Whites. Darks. Somebody's jeans and shirts stained with oil. There's towels and sheets and bras. There's a red-checked tablecloth. I flush the toilet for the sound effect.

There's no diapers or children's clothes.

In the living room, the chicken woman is still looking at the ceiling, only now she's shaking with long, jerking breaths. Her chest, under the apron, shaking. Helen is touching the corner of a folded tissue to the watery makeup. The tissue is soaked and black with mascara, and Helen's saying, "It will be better someday, Rhonda. You can't see that, but it will." Folding another tissue and daubing, she says, "What you have to do is make yourself hard. Think of yourself as something hard and sharp."

She says, "You're still a young woman, Rhonda. You need to go back to school and turn this hurt into money."

The chicken woman, Rhonda, is still crying with her head tilted back, staring at the ceiling.

Behind the bathroom, there's two bedrooms. One has a water bed. In the other bedroom is a crib and a hanging mobile of plastic daisies. There's a chest of drawers painted white. The crib is empty. The little plastic mattress is tied in a roll at one end. Near the crib is a stack of books on a stool. *Poems and Rhymes* is on top.

When I put the book on the dresser, it falls open to page 27.

I run the point of a baby pin down the inside edge of the page, tight in next to the binding, and the page pulls out. With the page folded in my pocket, I put the book back on the stack.

In the living room, the cosmetics are dumped in a heap on the floor.

Helen's pulled a false bottom out of the inside of her cosmetic case. Inside are layered necklaces and bracelets, heavy brooches and pairs of earrings clipped together, all of them crusted and dazzling with shattered red and green, yellow and blue lights. Jewels. Draped between Helen's hands is a long necklace of yellow and red stones larger than her polished, pink fingernails.

"In brilliant-cut diamonds," she says, "look for no light leakage through the facets below the girdle of the stone." She lays the necklace in the woman's hands, saying, "In rubies—aluminum oxide—foreign bits inside, called rutile inclusions, can give the stone a soft pinkish look unless the jeweler bakes the stone under high heat."

The trick to forgetting the big picture is to look at everything close-up.

The two women sit so close, their knees dovetail together. Their heads almost touch. The chicken woman isn't crying.

The chicken woman is wearing a jeweler's loupe in one eye.

The dead flowers are shoved aside, and scattered on the coffee table are clusters of sparkling pink and smooth gold, cool white pearls and carved blue lapis lazuli. Other clusters glow orange and yellow. Other piles shine silver and white.

And Helen cups a blazing green egg in her hand, so bright both women look green in the reflected light, and she says, "Do you see the kind of uniform veil-like inclusions in a synthetic emerald?"

Her eye clenched around the loupe, the woman nods.

And Helen says, "Remember this. I don't want you to get burned the way I was." She reaches into the cosmetic case and lifts out a bright handful of yellow, saying, "This yellow sapphire brooch was owned by the movie star Natasha Wren." With both hands, she takes out a sparkling pink heart, trailing a long chain of smaller diamonds, saying, "This seven-hundred-carat beryl pendant was once owned by Queen Marie of Romania."

In this heap of jewels, Helen Hoover Boyle would say, are the ghosts of everyone who has ever owned them. Everyone rich and successful enough to prove it. All of their talent and intelligence and beauty, outlived by decorative junk. All the success and accomplishment this jewelry was supposed to represent, it's all vanished.

With the same hairdo, the same makeup, leaning together so close, they could be sisters. They could be mother and daughter. Before and after. Past and future.

There's more, but that's when I go out to the car.

Sitting in the backseat, Mona says, "You find it?"

And I say yeah. Not that it does this woman any good.

The only thing we've given her is big hair and probably ring-worm.

Oyster says, "Show us the song. Let's see what this trip is all about."

And I tell him, no fucking way. I tuck the folded page in my mouth and chew and chew. My foot aches, and I take off my shoe. I chew and chew. Mona falls asleep. I chew and chew. Oyster looks out the window at some weeds in a ditch.

I swallow the page, and I fall asleep.

Later, sitting in the car, driving to the next town, the next library, maybe the next makeover, I wake up and Helen has been driving for almost three hundred miles.

It's almost dark, and just looking out the windshield, she says, "I'm keeping track of expenses."

Mona sits up, scratching her scalp through her hair. She presses the finger next to her pinkie finger, she presses the pad of that finger into the inside corner of her eye and pulls it away, fast, with an eye goober stuck on it. She wipes the goober on her jeans and says, "Where are we going to eat?"

I tell Mona to buckle her seat belt.

Helen turns on the headlights. She opens one hand, wide, against the steering wheel and looks at the back of it, her rings, and says, "After we find the Book of Shadows, when we're the all-powerful leaders of the entire world, after we're immortal and we own everything on the planet and everyone loves us," she says, "you'll still owe me for two hundred dollars' worth of cosmetics."

She looks odd. Her hair looks wrong. It's her earrings, the heavy clumps of pink and red, pink sapphires and rubies. They're gone.

Chapter 21

This wasn't just one night. It just feels that way. This was every night, through Texas and Arizona, on into Nevada, cutting through California and up through Oregon, Washington, Idaho, Montana. Every night, driving in a car is the same. Wherever.

Every place is the same place in the dark.

"My son, Patrick, isn't dead," Helen Hoover Boyle says.

He's dead in the county medical records, but I don't say anything.

With Helen driving, Mona and Oyster are asleep in the backseat. Asleep or listening. I sit in the passenger side of the front seat. Leaning against my door, I'm as far from Helen as I can get. With my head pillowed on my arm, I'm where I can listen without looking at her.

And Helen talks to me without looking back. This is both of us looking straight ahead at the road in the headlights rushing under the hood of the car.

"Patrick's at the New Continuum Medical Center," she says. "And I fully believe that someday he'll make a complete recovery."

Her daily planner book, bound in red leather, is on the front seat between us.

Driving through North Dakota and Minnesota, I ask, how did she find the culling spell?

And with one pink fingernail, she pushes a button somewhere in the dark and puts the car in cruise control. With something else in the dark, she turns on the high-beam headlights.

"I used to be a client representative for Skin Tone Cosmetics," she says. "The trailer we lived in wasn't very nice." She says, "My husband and I."

His name is John Boyle in the county medical records.

"You know how it is with your first," she says. "People give you so many toys and books. I don't even know who actually brought the book. It was just a book in a pile of books."

According to the county, this must've been twenty years ago.

"You don't need me to tell you what happened," she says. "But John always thought it was my fault."

According to police records, there were six domestic disturbance calls to the Boyle home, lot 175 at the Buena Noche Mobile Home Park, in the weeks following the death of Patrick Raymond Boyle, aged six months.

Driving through Wisconsin and Nebraska, Helen says, "I was going door-to-door, cold-calling for Skin Tone." She says, "I didn't go back to work right away. It must've been, God, a year and a half after Patrick's . . . after the morning we found Patrick."

She was walking around the trailer development where they lived, Helen tells me, and she met a young woman just like the woman wearing the apron patterned with little chickens. The same dead funeral flowers brought home from the mortuary. The same empty crib.

"I could make a lot of money just selling heavy foundation and cover-up," Helen says, smiling, "especially toward the end of the month, when money was tight."

Twenty years ago, this other woman was the same age as Helen, and while they talked, she showed Helen the nursery, the baby pictures. The woman's name was Cynthia Moore. She had a black eye.

"And I saw they had a copy of our same book," Helen says. *"Poems and Rhymes from Around the World."*

These other people kept it open to the same page it was the night their child died. The book, the bedding in the crib, they were trying to keep everything the same.

"Of course it was the same page as our book," Helen says.

At home John Boyle was drinking a lot of beer every night. He said he didn't want to have another child because he didn't trust her. If she didn't know what she'd done wrong, it was too much of a risk.

With my hand on her heated leather seats, it feels as if I'm touching another person.

Driving through Colorado, Kansas, and Missouri, she says, "The other mother in the trailer park, one day there was a yard sale at their place. All their baby things, all folded in piles on the lawn, marked a quarter apiece. There was the book, and I bought it." Helen says, "I asked the man inside why Cindy was selling everything, and he just shrugged."

According to county medical records, Cynthia Moore drank liquid drain cleaner and died of esophageal hemorrhaging and asphyxiation three months after her child had died of no apparent cause.

"John was worried about germs so he'd burned all of Patrick's things," she says. "I bought the book of poems for ten cents. I remember it was a beautiful day outside."

Police records show three more domestic disturbance calls to lot 175 at the Buena Noche Mobile Home Park. A week after

Cynthia Moore's suicide, John Boyle was found dead of no apparent cause. According to the county, his high blood alcohol concentration might've caused sleep apnea. Another likely cause was positional asphyxiation. He may have been so drunk that he fell unconscious in a position that kept him from breathing. Either way, there were no marks on the body. There was no apparent cause of death on the death certificate.

Driving through Illinois, Indiana, and Ohio, Helen says, "Killing John wasn't anything I did on purpose." She says, "I was just curious."

The same as me and Duncan.

"I was just testing a theory," she says. "John kept saying that Patrick's ghost was with us. And I kept telling him that Patrick was still alive in the hospital."

Twenty years later, baby Patrick's still in the hospital, she says.

Crazy as this sounds, I don't say anything. How a baby must look after twenty years in a coma or on life support or whatever, I can't imagine.

Picture Oyster on a feeding tube and a catheter for most of his life.

There are worse things you can do to the people you love than kill them.

In the backseat, Mona sits up and stretches her arms. She says, "In ancient Greece, people wrote their strongest curses with the nails from shipwrecks." She says, "Sailors who died at sea weren't given a proper funeral. The Greeks knew that dead people who aren't buried are the most restless and destructive spirits."

And Helen says, "Shut up."

Driving through West Virginia, Pennsylvania, and New York, Helen says, "I hate people who claim they can see ghosts." She says, "There are no ghosts. When you die, you're dead. There's no afterlife. People who claim they can see ghosts are just looking for attention. People who believe in reincarnation are just postponing their lives."

She smiles. "Fortunately for me," she says, "I've found a way to punish those people and make a great deal of money."

Her cell phone rings.

She says, "If you don't believe me about Patrick, I can show you this month's hospital bill."

Her phone rings again.

We're driving across Vermont when she says this. She says part of it while we're crossing Louisiana in the dark, then Arkansas and Mississippi. All those little eastern states, some nights, we'd cross two or three.

Flipping her phone open, she says, "This is Helen." She rolls her eyes at me and says, "An invisible baby sealed inside your bedroom wall? And it cries all night? Really?"

Other parts of this story, I didn't know until we got home and I did some research.

Pressing the phone against her chest, Helen tells me, "Everything I'm telling you is strictly off the record." She says, "Until we find the Book of Shadows, we can't change what's happened. Using a spell from that book, I'll make sure Patrick makes a full recovery."

Chapter 22

We're driving through the Midwest with the radio on some AM station, and a man's voice says how Dr. Sara Lowenstein was a beacon of hope and morality in the wasteland of modern life. Dr. Sara was a noble, hard-line moralist who refused to accept anything but steadfast righteous conduct. She was a bastion of upright standards, a lamp that shone its light to reveal the evil of this world. Dr. Sara, the man says, will always be in our hearts and souls because her own soul was so strong and so un——

The voice stops.

And Mona hits the back of the front seat, hits right behind my kidneys, and says, "Not again." She says, "Quit venting your personal issues on innocent people."

And I say for her to stop accusing. Maybe it's just sunspots.

These talk-oholics. These listen-ophobics.

The culling song's spun through my head so fast I didn't even notice. I was half asleep. It's that far out of control. I can kill in my sleep.

After a few miles of silence, what radio journalists call dead air, another man's voice comes on the radio, saying how Dr. Sara Lowenstein was the moral yardstick against which millions of radio listeners measured their own lives. She was the flaming sword of God, sent down to route the misdeeds and evildoers from the temple of——

And this new man's voice cuts off.

Mona hits the back of my seat, hard, saying, "That's not funny. Those radio preachers are real people!"

And I say, I didn't do anything.

And Helen and Oyster giggle.

Mona crosses her arms over her chest and throws herself back against the rear seat. She says, "You have no respect. None. This is a million years of power you're screwing around with."

Mona puts both hands against Oyster and shoves him away, hard, so he hits the door. She says, "You, too." She says, "A radio personality is just as important as a cow or a pig."

Now dance music comes on the radio. Helen's cell phone starts to ring, and she flips it open and presses it into her hair. She nods at the radio and mouths the words *Turn it down*.

Into the phone, she says, "Yes." She says, "Uh-huh, yes, I know who he is. Tell me where he's at right now, as close as you can pinpoint it."

I turn down the radio.

Helen listens and says, "No." She says, "I want a seventy-five-carat fancy-cut blue-white diamond. Call Mr. Drescher in Geneva, he knows the exact one I want."

Mona pulls her knapsack up from the floor of the backseat, and she takes out a pack of colored felt-tip pens and a thick book, bound in dark green brocade. She opens the book across her lap and starts scribbling in it with a blue pen. She caps the blue pen and starts with a yellow one.

And Helen says, "How much security doesn't matter. It'll be done inside the hour." She flips the phone shut and drops it on the seat beside her.

On the front seat, between us, is her daily planner, and she flips it open and writes a name and today's date inside.

The book in Mona's lap is her Mirror Book. All real witches, she says, keep Mirror Books. It's a kind of diary and cookbook where you collect what you learn about magic and rituals.

"For instance," she says, reading from her Mirror Book, "Democritus says that burning the head of a chameleon on an oak fire will cause a thunderstorm."

She leans forward and says right into my ear, "You know, Democritus," she says, "like in the inventor of *democracy*."

And I'm counting 1, counting 2, counting 3 . . .

To shut someone up, Mona says, to make them stop talking, take a fish and sew its mouth shut.

To cure an earache, Mona says, you need to use the semen of a boar as it drips from a sow's vagina.

According to the Jewish *Sepher ha-Razim* collection of spells, you have to kill a black puppy before it sees the light of day. Then write your curse on a tablet and put the tablet inside the dog's head. Then seal the mouth with wax and hide the head behind someone's house, and that person will never fall asleep.

"According to Theophrastus," Mona reads, "you should only dig up a peony at night because if a woodpecker sees you doing it, you'll go blind. If the woodpecker sees you cutting the plant's roots, your anus will prolapse."

And Helen says, "I wish I had a fish . . ."

According to Mona, you shouldn't kill people, because that drives you away from humanity. In order to justify killing, you have to make the victim your enemy. To justify any crime, you have to make the victim your enemy.

After long enough, everyone in the world will be your enemy.

With every crime, Mona says, you're more and more alienated from the world. More and more, you imagine the whole world is against you.

"Dr. Sara Lowenstein didn't start out by attacking and berating everybody who called her radio show," Mona says. "She used to have a little time slot and a little audience, and she seemed to really care about helping people."

And maybe it was after years and years of getting the same calls about unwanted pregnancies, about divorces, about family squabbles. Maybe it was because her audience grew and her show moved to prime time. Maybe it was the more money she earned. Maybe power corrupts, but she wasn't always a bitch.

The only way out, Mona says, will be to surrender and let the world kill Helen and me for our crimes. Or we can kill ourselves.

I ask if this is more Wiccan nonsense.

And Mona says, "No, actually, it's Karl Marx."

She says, "After killing someone, those are the only ways back to connect with humanity." Still drawing in her book, she says, "That's the only way you can get back to a place where the world isn't your nemesis. Where you're not totally alone."

"A fish," Helen says, "and a needle and thread."

And I'm not alone.

I have Helen.

Maybe this is why so many serial killers work in pairs. It's nice not to feel alone in a world full of victims or enemies. It's no wonder Waltraud Wagner, the Austrian Angel of Death, convinced her friends to kill with her.

It just seems natural.

You and me against the world . . .

Gary Lewingdon had his brother, Thaddeus. Kenneth Bianchi had Angelo Buono. Larry Bittaker had Roy Norris. Doug Clark had Carol Bundy. David Gore had Fred Waterfield. Gwen Graham had Cathy Wood. Doug Gretzler had Bill Steelman. Joe Kallinger had his son, Mike. Pat Kearney had Dave Hill. Andy Kokoraleis had his brother, Tom. Leo Lake had Charles Ng. Henry Lucas had Ottis Toole. Albert Anselmi had John Scalise. Allen Michael had Cleamon Johnson. Clyde Barrow had Bonnie Parker. Doug Bemore had Keith Cosby. Ian Brady had Myra Hindley. Tom Braun had Leo Maine. Ben Brooks had Fred Treesh. John Brown had Sam Coetzee. Bill Burke had Bill Hare. Erskine Burrows had Larry Tacklyn. Jose Bux had Mariano Macu. Bruce Childs had Henry McKenny. Alton Coleman had Debbie Brown. Ann French had her son, Bill. Frank Gusenberg had his brother, Peter. Delfina Gonzalez had her sister, Maria. Dr. Teet Haerm had Dr. Tom Allgen. Amelia Sachs had Annie Walters.

Thirteen percent of all reported serial killers worked in teams.

On death row in San Quentin, Randy "the Scorecard Killer" Kraft played bridge with Doug "Sunset Slayer" Clark, Larry "Pliers" Bittaker, and Freeway Killer Bill Bonin. An estimated 126 victims between the four of them.

Helen Hoover Boyle has me.

"I couldn't stop killing," Bonin once told a reporter. "It got easier with each one . . ."

I have to agree. It does get to be a bad habit.

On the radio, it says how Dr. Sara Lowenstein was an angel of unparalleled power and impact, a glorious hand of God, a conscience for the world around her, a world of sin and cruel intent, a world of hidd——

The more people die, the more things stay the same.

"Go ahead, prove yourself," Oyster says, and nods at the radio. He says, "Kill this fucker, too."

I'm counting 37, counting 38, counting 39 . . .

We've disarmed seven copies of the poems book since leaving home. The original press run was 500. That makes it 306 copies down, 194 copies to go.

In the newspaper, it says how the man in the black leather trench coat, the one who shoved past me at the crosswalk, he was a monthly blood donor. He spent three years overseas with the Peace Corps, digging wells for lepers. He gave up a chunk of his liver to a girl in Botswana who ate a poison mushroom. He answered phones during pledge drives against some crippling disease, I forget what.

Still, he deserved to die. *He called me an asshole.*

He pushed me!

In the newspaper, it shows the mother and father crying over the coffin of my upstairs neighbor.

Still, *his stereo was too damn loud.*

In the newspaper, it says a cover girl fashion model named Denni D'Testro was found dead in her downtown loft apartment this morning.

And for whatever reason, I hope Nash didn't get the call to pick up the body.

Oyster points at the radio and says, "Kill him, Dad, or you're full of shit."

Really, this whole world is nothing but assholes.

Helen flips open her cell phone and calls ahead to libraries in Oklahoma and Florida. She finds another copy of the poems book in Orlando.

Mona reads to us how the ancient Greeks made curse tablets they called *defixiones.*

The Greeks used *kolossi,* dolls made of bronze or wax or clay, and they stabbed them with nails or twisted and mutilated them, cutting off the head or hands. They put hair from the victim inside the doll or sealed a curse, written on papyrus and rolled, inside the doll.

In the Louvre Museum is an Egyptian figure from the second century A.D. It's a naked woman, hog-tied, with nails stuck in her eyes, her ears, her mouth, breasts, hands, feet, vagina, and anus.

Scribbling in her book with an orange felt-tip pen, Mona says, "Whoever made that doll, they'd probably love you and Helen."

The curse tablets were thin sheets of lead or copper, sometimes clay. You wrote your curse on them with the nail from a shipwreck, then you rolled the sheet and stuck the nail through it. When writing, you wrote the first line left to right, the next line right to left, the third left to right, and so on. If you could, you folded the curse around some of the victim's hair or a scrap of their clothing. You threw the curse into a lake or a well or the sea, anything that would convey it to the underworld where demons would read it and fill your order.

Still talking on her phone, Helen puts it against her chest for a moment and says, "That sounds like ordering stuff over the Internet."

I'm counting 346, counting 347, counting 348...

In the Greco-Roman literary tradition, Mona says, there are night witches and day witches. Day witches are good and nurturing. Night witches are secretive and bent on destroying all civilization.

Mona says, "You two are definitely night witches."

These people who gave us democracy and architecture, Mona says magic was an everyday part of their lives. Businessmen put curses on each other. Neighbors cursed neighbors. Near the site of the original Olympic Games, archaeologists have found old wells full of curses placed by athletes on other athletes.

Mona says, "I'm not making this stuff up."

Spells to attract a lover were called *agogai* in ancient Greek.

Curses to ruin a relationship were called *diakopoi.*

Helen talks louder into her cell phone, saying, "Blood running down your kitchen walls? Well, of course you shouldn't have to live with that."

And into his phone, Oyster says, "I need the retail advertising number for the *Miami Telegraph-Observer.*"

And the radio interrupts everything with a chorus of French horns. A man's deep voice comes on with a Teletype clattering in the background.

"The suspected leader of South America's largest drug cartel has been found dead in his Miami penthouse," the voice says. "Gustave Brennan, aged thirty-nine, is believed to be the point man for almost three billion dollars in annual cocaine sales. Police do not have a cause of death, but plan to autopsy the body . . ."

And Helen looks at the radio and says, "Are you hearing this? This is ridiculous." She says, "Listen," and turns up the radio.

". . . Brennan," the voice says, "who lived inside a fortress of armed bodyguards, has also been under constant FBI surveillance . . ."

And to me, Helen says, "Do they even use Teletypes anymore?"

The call she just got—the blue-white diamond—the name she wrote in her daily planner, it was Gustave Brennan.

Chapter 23

Centuries ago, sailors on long voyages used to leave a pair of pigs on every deserted island. Or they'd leave a pair of goats. Either way, on any future visit, the island would be a source of meat. These islands, they were pristine. These were home to breeds of birds with no natural predators. Breeds of birds that lived nowhere else on earth. The plants there, without enemies they evolved without thorns or poisons. Without predators and enemies, these islands, they were paradise.

The sailors, the next time they visited these islands, the only things still there would be herds of goats or pigs.

Oyster is telling this story.

The sailors called this "seeding meat."

Oyster says, "Does this remind you of anything? Maybe the ol' Adam and Eve story?"

Looking out the car window, he says, "You ever wonder when God's coming back with a lot of barbecue sauce?"

Outside is some Great Lake, water stretched to the horizon, nothing but zebra mussels and lamprey eels, Oyster says. The air stinks with rotting fish.

Mona has a pillow of barley and lavender pressed over her face with both hands. The red henna designs on the back of her hands spread down the length of each finger. Red snakes and vines twisted together.

His cell phone rings, and Oyster pulls out the antenna. He puts it to his head and says, "Deemer, Davis and Hope, Attorneys-at-Law."

He twists a finger in his nose, then takes it out and looks at the finger. Into his phone, Oyster says, "How long after eating there did the diarrhea manifest itself?" He sees me looking and flicks the finger at me.

Helen, with her own cell phone, says, "The people who lived there before were very happy. It's a beautiful house."

In the local newspaper, the *Erie Register-Sentinel*, an ad in the Entertainment section says:

Attention Patrons of the Country House Golf Club

The ad says: "Have you contracted a medication-resistant staph infection from the swimming pool or locker room facilities? If so, please call the following number to be part of a class-action lawsuit."

You know the number is Oyster's cell phone.

In the 1870s, Oyster says, a man named Spencer Baird decided to play God. He decided the cheapest form of protein for Americans was the European carp. For twenty years, he shipped baby carp to every part of the country. He convinced a hundred different railroads to carry his baby carp and release them in every body of water their trains passed. He even outfitted special railroad tanker cars that carried nine-ton shipments of baby carp to every watershed in North America.

Helen's phone rings and she flips it open. Her daily planner open on the seat next to her, she says, "And where exactly is His Royal Highness at this time?" and she writes a name under to-day's date in the book. Into her phone, Helen says, "Ask Mr. Drescher to get me the pair of citron and emerald clips."

In another newspaper, the *Cleveland Herald-Monitor*, in the Lifestyles section is an ad that says:

Attention Patrons of the Apparel-Design Chain of Clothing Stores

The ad says: "If you've contracted genital herpes while trying on clothing, please call the following number to be part of a class-action lawsuit."

And, again, the same number. Oyster's number.

In 1890, Oyster says, another man decided to play God. Eugene Schieffelin released sixty *Sturnus vulgaris*, the European starling, in New York's Central Park. Fifty years later, the birds had spread to San Francisco. Today, there are more than 200 million starlings in America. All this because Schieffelin wanted the New World to include every bird mentioned by Shakespeare.

And into his cell phone, Oyster says, "No, sir, your name will be held in strictest confidence."

Helen flips her phone shut, and she cups a gloved hand over her nose and mouth, saying, "What is that awful smell?"

And Oyster puts his cell phone against his shirt and says, "Alewife die-off."

Ever since they reengineered the Welland Canal in 1921 to al-low more shipping around Niagara Falls, he says, the sea lamprey has infested all the Great Lakes. These parasites suck the blood of the larger fish, the trout and salmon, killing them. Then the smaller fish are left with no predators and their population explodes. Then they run out of plankton to eat, and starve by the millions.

"Stupid greedy alewives," Oyster says. "Remind you of any other species?"

He says, "Either a species learns to control its own population, or something like disease, famine, war, will take care of the issue."

Mona's muffled voice through her pillow, she says, "Don't tell them. They won't understand."

And Helen opens her purse on the seat beside her. She opens it with one hand and takes out a polished cylinder. With the air-conditioning on high, she sprays breath freshener on a handkerchief and holds it over her nose. She sprays breath freshener into the air-conditioning vents, and says, "Is this about the culling poem?"

And without turning around, I say, "You'd use the poem for population control?"

And Oyster laughs and says, "Kind of."

Mona lowers the pillow to her lap and says, "This is about the grimoire."

And punching another number into his cell phone, Oyster says, "If we find it, we all have to share it."

And I say, we're destroying it.

"After we read it," Helen says.

And into his phone, Oyster says, "Yes, I'll hold." And to us, he says, "This is so typical. We have the entire power structure of Western society in this one car."

According to Oyster, the "dads" have all the power so they don't want anything to change.

He means me.

I'm counting 1, counting 2, counting 3 . . .

Oyster says all the "moms" have a little power, but they're hungry for more.

He means Helen.

I'm counting 4, counting 5, counting 6 . . .

And young people, he says, have little or no power so they're desperate for any.

Oyster and Mona.

I'm counting 7, counting 8 . . . , and Oyster's voice goes on and on.

This quiet-ophobic. This talk-oholic.

Smiling with just half his mouth, Oyster says, "Every generation wants to be the last." Into the phone, he says, "Yeah, I'd like to place a retail display ad." He says, "Yeah, I'll hold."

Mona puts the pillow back over her face. The red snakes and vines go down the length of each finger.

Cheatgrass, Oyster says. Mustard. Kudzu.

Carp. Starlings. Seeding meat.

Looking out the car window, Oyster says, "You ever wonder if Adam and Eve were just the puppies God dumped because they wouldn't house-train?"

He rolls down the window and the smell blows inside, the stinking warm wind of dead fish, and shouting against the wind, he says, "Maybe humans are just the pet alligators that God flushed down the toilet."

Chapter 24

At the next library, I ask to wait in the car while Helen and Mona go inside and find the book. With them gone, I flip through the pages of Helen's daily planner. Almost every day is a name, some of them names I know. The dictator of some banana republic or a figure from organized crime. Each name crossed out with a single red slash. The last dozen names I write on a scrap of paper. Between the names are Helen's notes for meetings, her handwriting scrolled and perfect as jewelry.

Watching me from the backseat, Oyster's kicked back with his arms folded behind his head. His bare feet are crossed and propped up on the back of the front seat so they hang next to my face. A silver ring around one of his big toes. Calluses on the soles, the gray calluses are cracked, dirty, and Oyster says, "Mom's not going to like that, you going through her personal secret shit."

Reading the book backward from today's date, I go through three years of names, assassinations, before Helen and Mona are walking back through the parking lot.

Oyster's phone rings, and he answers it, "Donner, Diller and Dunes, Attorneys-at-Law . . ."

There's still most of the book I don't get a chance to read. Years and years of pages. Toward the end of the book, there are years and years of blank pages for Helen still to fill.

Helen's talking on her phone when she gets to the car. She's saying, "No, I want the step-cut aquamarine that used to belong to the Emperor Zog."

Mona gets into the backseat, saying, "Did you miss us?" She says, "Another culling song down the toilet."

And Oyster folds his legs into the backseat, saying, "Does the rash bleed?" into his cell phone.

Helen snaps her fingers for me to hand her the daily planner. Into the phone, she says, "Yes, the two-hundred-carat aquamarine. Call Drescher in Geneva." She opens the planner and writes a name under today's date.

Mona says, "I was thinking." She says, "Do you think the original grimoire might have a flying spell? I'd love that. Or an invisibility spell?" She gets her Mirror Book out of her knapsack and starts coloring in it. She says, "I want to be able to talk to animals, too. Oh, and do telekinesis, you know, move stuff with my mind . . ."

Helen starts the car and says, loud at the rearview mirror, "I'm sewing my fish."

She puts her cell phone and her pen in her purse. Still in her purse is the small gray stone from Mona's witch party, the stone the coven gave to her. When Oyster was naked. His wrinkled pink stalactite of skin pierced with its little silver ring.

Mona, that same night, Mulberry, and the two muscles of her back, the way they split into the two firm, creamy white halves of her ass, and I'm counting 1, counting 2, counting 3 . . .

In the next little town, in the next library, I ask Helen and Mona to wait in the car with Oyster while I go inside and hunt for the poems book.

This is some small-town library in the middle of the day. A librarian is behind the checkout desk. The most recent newspapers are mounted in big hardcover bindings you sit at a big table to read. In today's paper is Gustave Brennan. In yesterday's is some wacko religious leader in the Middle East. Two days ago, it was some death row inmate on his latest appeal.

Everyone in Helen's planner book died on the date their name is listed.

In between are newspaper articles about something worse. Denni D'Testro today. Three days ago, it's Samantha Evian. A week ago, it's Dot Leine. All of them young, all of them fashion models, all of them found dead without an apparent cause of death. Before that was Mimi Gonzalez, found dead by her boyfriend, dead in bed with no marks, nothing. No clues until the autopsy announced today shows signs of post-mortem sexual intercourse.

Nash.

Helen comes in, asking, "I'm hungry. What's taking you so long?"

My list of names is on the table beside me. Next to that is a newspaper article with a photo of Gustave Brennan. In front of me is another article showing the funeral of some convicted child molester I found listed in Helen's daily planner.

And Helen looks at everything in one glance and says, "So now you know."

She sits on the edge of the table, her thighs stretching her skirt tight across her lap, and she says, "You wanted to know how to control your power, well, this is what works for me."

The secret is to turn pro, she says. Do something only for money, and you're less likely to do it for free. "You don't think prostitutes want a lot of sex outside of their brothel?" she says.

She says, "Why do you think building contractors always live in unfinished houses?"

She says, "Why do you think doctors are in such poor health?"

She waves her hand at the library door and the parking lot outside and says, "The only reason why I haven't killed Mona a hundred times over is because I kill someone else every day. And I get paid a great deal of money for it."

And I ask, what about Mona's idea? Why can't you control the power by just loving people so much you don't want to kill them?

"This isn't about love and hate," Helen says. It's about control. People don't sit down and read a poem to kill their child. They just want the child to sleep. They just want to dominate. No matter how much you love someone, you still want to have your own way.

The masochist bullies the sadist into action. The most passive person is actually an aggressor. Every day, just you living means the misery and death of plants and animals—and even some people. "Slaughterhouses, factory farms, sweatshops," she says, "like it or not, that's what your money buys."

And I tell her she's been listening to Oyster too much.

"The key is to kill people deliberately," Helen says, and picks up the picture of Gustave Brennan in the newspaper. Looking at it, up close, she says, "You kill strangers deliberately so you don't accidentally kill the people you love."

Constructive destruction.

She says, "I'm an independent contractor."

She's an international hired killer working for huge diamonds.

Helen says, "Governments do it every day."

But governments do it after years of deliberation and by due process, I tell her. It's only after weighty consideration that a criminal is deemed too dangerous to be released. Or to set an example. Or for revenge. Okay, so the process isn't perfect. At least it's not arbitrary.

And Helen puts a hand over her eyes to hide them for a moment, then moves her hand and looks at me, saying, "Who do you think calls me for these little jobs?"

The U.S. State Department calls her?

"Sometimes," she says. "Mostly it's other countries, any country in the world, but I don't do anything for free."

That's why the jewels?

"I *hate* haggling over the exchange rate, don't you?" she says. "Besides, an animal dies for every meal you eat."

Oyster again. I see my job will be keeping him and Helen apart.

And I say, that's different. Humans are above animals. Animals were put on this planet to feed and serve humanity. Human beings are precious and intelligent and unique, and God gave the animals to us. They're our property.

"Of course you'd say that," Helen says, "you're on the winning team."

I say, constructive destruction isn't the answer I was looking for.

And Helen says, "Sorry, it's the only one I have."

She says, "Let's get the book, fix it, and then go kill ourselves some lovely pheasant for lunch."

On the way out, I ask the librarian for their copy of the poems book. But it's checked out. The details about the librarian are he has frosted streaks of ash blond in his hair, and the hair's gelled into a solid awning over his face. Sort of an ash-blond visor. He's sitting on a stool behind a computer monitor and smells like cigarette smoke. He's wearing a turtleneck sweater with a plastic name tag that says, "Symon."

I tell him that a lot of lives depend on me finding that book.

And he says, too bad.

And I say, no, the fact is only *his* life depends on it.

And the librarian hits a button on his keyboard and says he's calling the police.

"Wait," Helen says, and spreads her hand on the counter, her fingers sparkling and loaded with step-cut emeralds and cabochon star sapphires and black, cushion-cut bort diamonds. She says, "Symon, take your pick."

And the librarian, his top lip sucks up to his nose so his upper teeth show. He blinks, once, twice, slow, and he says, "Honey, you can keep your tacky drag queen rhinestones."

And the smile on Helen's face doesn't even flicker.

The man's eyes roll up, and the muscles in his face and hands go smooth. His chin drops to his chest, and he slumps forward against his keyboard, then twists and slides to the floor.

Constructive destruction.

Helen reaches a priceless hand to turn the monitor and says, "Damn."

Even dead on the floor, he looks asleep. His giant gelled hair broke his fall.

Reading the monitor, Helen says, "He changed the screen. I need to know his password."

No problem. Big Brother fills us all with the same crap. My guess is he was clever the same way everybody thinks they're clever. I tell her to type in "password."

Chapter 25

Mona rolls the sock off my foot. The stretchy sock insides, the fibers, they peel my scabs off. My crusted blood flakes off onto the floor. The foot is swollen until it's smooth with all its wrinkles stretched out. My foot, a balloon spotted red and yellow. With a folded towel under it, Mona pours the rubbing alcohol.

The pain's so instant you can't tell if the alcohol is boiling hot or ice cold. Sitting on the motel bed, my pant leg rolled up, with Mona kneeling on the carpet at my feet, I grab two handfuls of bedspread and grit my teeth. My back arched, my every muscle bunches tight for a few long seconds. The bedspread's cold and soaked with my sweat.

Pockets of something soft and yellow, these blisters almost cover the bottom of my foot. Under the layer of dead skin, you can see a dark, solid shape inside each blister.

Mona says, "What've you been walking on?"

She's heating a pair of tweezers over Oyster's plastic cigarette lighter.

I ask what the deal is with the advertisements Oyster's running in newspapers. Is he working for a law firm? The outbreaks of skin fungus and food poisoning, are they for real?

The alcohol drips off my foot, pink with dissolved blood, onto the folded motel towel. She sets the tweezers on the damp towel and heats a needle over Oyster's cigarette lighter. With a rubber band, she reaches back and bundles her hair into a thick ponytail.

"Oyster calls all that 'antiadvertising,'" she says. "Sometimes businesses, the really rich ones, they pay him to cancel the ads. How much they pay, he says, reflects how true the ads probably are."

My foot won't fit inside my shoe anymore. In the car, earlier today, I asked if Mona could look at it. Helen and Oyster are out buying new makeup. They're stopping to defuse three copies of the poems book at a big used-book store down the street. The Book Barn.

I say what Oyster's doing is blackmail. It's casting aspersions.

Now it's almost midnight. Where Helen and Oyster really are I don't want to know.

"He's not saying he's a lawyer," Mona says. "He's not saying there's a lawsuit. He's just running an ad. Other people fill in the blanks. Oyster says he's just planting the seed of doubt in their minds."

She says, "Oyster says it's only fair since advertising promises something to make you happy."

With her kneeling, you can see the three black stars tattooed above Mona's collarbone. You can see down her blouse, past the carpet of chains and pendants, and she isn't wearing a bra, and I'm counting 1, counting 2, counting 3 . . .

Mona says, "Other members of the coven do it, too, but it's Oyster's idea. He says the plan is to undermine the illusion of safety and comfort in people's lives."

With the needle, she lances a yellow blister and something drops out. A little brown piece of plastic, it's covered in stinking ooze and blood and lands on the towel. Mona turns it over with the needle, and the yellow ooze soaks into the towel. She picks it up with the tweezers and says, "What the heck is this?"

It's a church steeple.

I say, I don't know.

Mona, her mouth gaps open with her tongue pushing out. Her throat slides up inside her neck skin, gagging. She waves a hand in front of her nose and blinks fast. The yellow ooze stinks that bad. She wipes the needle on the towel. With one hand she holds my toes, and with the other she lances another blister. The yellow sprays out in a little blast, and there on the towel is half of a factory smokestack.

She tweezers it and wipes it on the towel. Her face wrinkled tight around her nose, she looks at it close-up and says, "You want to tell me what's going on?"

She lances another blister, and out pops the onion dome from a mosque, covered in blood and slime. With her tweezers, Mona pulls a tiny dinner plate out of my foot. It's hand-painted with a border of red roses.

Outside our motel room, a fire siren screams by in the street.

Out of another blister oozes the pediment from a Georgian bank building.

The cupola from a grade school busts out of the next blister.

Sweating. Deep breathing. Gripping my soft, dripping handfuls of bedspread, I grit my teeth. Looking up at the ceiling, I say, someone is killing models.

Pulling out a bloody flying buttress, Mona says, "By stepping on them?"

And I tell her, *fashion* models.

The needle digs around in the sole of my foot. The needle fishes out a television antenna. The tweezers fish out a gargoyle. Then roof tiles, shingles, tiny slates and gutters.

Mona lifts one edge of the stinking towel and folds it so a clean side shows. She pours on more alcohol.

Another fire engine screams by the motel. Its red and blue lights flash across the curtains.

And I can't draw another full breath, my foot burns so bad.

We need, I say. I need . . . we need . . .

We need to go back home, I say, as soon as possible. If I'm right, I need to stop the man who's using the culling poem.

With the tweezers, Mona digs out a blue plastic shutter and lays it on the towel. She pulls out a shred of bedroom curtains, yellow curtains from the nursery. She pulls out a length of picket fence, and pours on more alcohol until it drips off my foot clear. She covers her nose with her hand.

Another fire engine screams by, and Mona says, "You mind if I just turn on the TV and see what's up?"

I stretch my jaws at the ceiling and say, we can't . . . we can't . . .

Alone with her now, I say, we can't trust Helen. She only wants the grimoire so she can control the world. I say, the cure for having too much power is not to get more power. We can't let Helen get her hands on the original Book of Shadows.

And so slow I can't see her move, Mona draws a fluted Ionic column out of a bloody pit below my big toe. Slow as the hour hand on a clock. If the column's from a museum or a church or a college, I can't remember. All these broken homes and trashed institutions.

She's more of an archaeologist than a surgeon.

And Mona says, "That's funny."

She lines up the column with the other fragments on the towel. Frowning as she leans back into my sole with the tweezers, she says, "Helen told me the same thing about you. She says you only want to destroy the grimoire."

It should be destroyed. No one can handle that kind of power.

On television is an old brick building, three stories, with flames pouring up from every window. Firemen point hoses and feathery white arcs of water. A young man holding a microphone steps into the shot, and behind him Helen and Oyster are watch-

154

ing the fire, their heads leaned together. Oyster's holding a shopping bag. Helen holds his other hand.

Holding up the bottle of rubbing alcohol, Mona looks at how much is left. She says, "What I'd really like to be is an empath, where all I have to do is touch people and they're healed." Reading the label, she says, "Helen tells me we can make the world a paradise."

I sit up on the bed, halfway, propping myself on my elbows, and I say, Helen is killing people for diamond tiaras. That's the kind of savior Helen is.

Mona wipes the tweezers and the needle on the towel, making more smears of red and yellow. She smells the bottle of alcohol and says, "Helen thinks you only want to exploit the book for a newspaper story. She says once all the spells are destroyed—including the culling spell—then you can blab to everybody that you're the hero."

I say, nuclear weapons are bad enough. Chemical weapons. I say, certain people having magic is not going to make the world a better place.

I tell Mona, if it comes to it, I'll need her help.

I say, we may need to kill Helen.

And Mona shakes her head over the bloody ruins on the motel towel. She says, "So your answer for too much killing is more killing?"

Just Helen, I say. And maybe Nash, if my theory about the dead fashion models is right. After we kill them, we can go back to normal.

On television, the young man with the microphone, he's saying how a three-alarm fire has most of the downtown area paralyzed. He says, the structure is fully involved. He says, it's one of the city's favorite institutions.

"Oyster," Mona says, "doesn't like your idea of normal."

The burning institution, it's the Book Barn. And behind him, Helen and Oyster are gone.

Mona says, "In a detective story, do you wonder why we root for the detective to win?" She says, maybe it's not just for revenge or to stop the killing. Maybe we really want to see the killer redeemed. The detective is the killer's savior. Imagine if Jesus chased you around, trying to catch you and save your soul. Not just a patient passive God, but a hardworking, aggressive bloodhound. We want the criminal to confess during the trial. We want him to be exposed in the drawing room scene, surrounded by his peers. The detective is a shepherd, and we want the criminal back in the fold, returned to us. We love him. We miss him. We want to hug him.

Mona says, "Maybe that's why so many women marry killers in prison. To help heal them."

I tell her, there's nobody who misses me.

Mona shakes her head and says, "You know, you and Helen are so much like my parents."

Mona. Mulberry. My daughter.

And flopping back on the bed, I ask, how's that?

And pulling a door frame out of my foot, Mona says, "Just this morning, Helen told me she might need to kill you."

My pager goes off. It's a number I don't know. The pager says it's very important.

And Mona digs a stained-glass window out of a bloody pit in my foot. She holds it up so the ceiling light comes through the colored bits, and looking at the tiny window, she says, "I'm more worried about Oyster. He doesn't always tell the truth."

And the motel room door, right then it blows open. The sirens outside. The sirens on the television. The flash of red and blue lights strobing across the window curtains. Right then Helen and Oyster fall into the room, laughing and panting. Oyster slinging a bag of cosmetics. Helen holding her high heels in one hand. They both smell like Scotch whisky and smoke.

Chapter 26

I magine a plague you catch through your ears.

Oyster and his tree-hugging, eco-bullshit, his bio-invasive, apocryphal bullshit. The virus of his information. What used to be a beautiful deep green jungle to me, it's now a tragedy of English ivy choking everything else to death. The lovely shining black flocks of starlings, with their creepy whistling songs, they rob the nests of a hundred different native birds.

Imagine an idea that occupies your mind the way an army occupies a city.

Outside the car now is America.

Oh, beautiful starling-filled skies,
Over amber waves of tansy ragwort.

Oh, purple mountains of loosestrife,
Above the bubonic-plagued plain.

America.

A siege of ideas. The whole power grab of life.

After listening to Oyster, a glass of milk isn't just a nice drink with chocolate chip cookies. It's cows forced to stay pregnant and pumped with hormones. It's the inevitable calves that live a few miserable months, squeezed in veal boxes. A pork chop means a pig, stabbed and bleeding, with a snare around one foot, being hung up to die screaming as it's sectioned into chops and roasts and lard. Even a hard-boiled egg is a hen with her feet crippled from living in a battery cage only four inches wide, so narrow she can't raise her wings, so maddening her beak is cut off so she won't attack the hens trapped on each side of her. With her feathers rubbed off by the cage and her beak cut, she lays egg after egg until her bones are so depleted of calcium that they shatter at the slaughterhouse.

This is the chicken in chicken noodle soup, the laying hens, the hens so bruised and scarred that they have to be shredded and cooked because nobody would ever buy them in a butcher's case. This is the chicken in corn dogs. Chicken nuggets.

This is all Oyster talks about. This is his plague of information. This is when I turn on the radio, to country and western music. To basketball. Anything, so long as it's loud and constant and lets me pretend my breakfast sandwich is just a breakfast sandwich. That an animal is just that. An egg is just an egg. Cheese isn't a tiny suffering veal. That eating this is my right as a human being.

Here's Big Brother singing and dancing so I don't start thinking too much for my own good.

In the local newspaper today, there's another dead fashion model. There's an ad that says:

Attention Patrons of Falling Star Puppy Farm

It says: "If your new dog spreads infectious rabies to any child in your household, you may be eligible to take part in a class-action lawsuit."

Driving through what used to be beautiful, natural country, while eating what used to be an egg sandwich, I ask why they couldn't just buy the three books they were shopping for at the Book Barn. Oyster and Helen. Or just steal the pages and leave the rest of the books. I say, the reason we're making this trip is so people *won't* be burning books.

"Relax," Helen says, driving. "The store had three copies of the book. The problem was they didn't know where."

And Oyster says, "They were all misshelved." Mona's head is asleep in his lap, and he's peeling apart the strands of her hair into skeins of red and black. "It's the only way she falls asleep," he says. "She'd sleep forever if I kept doing this."

For whatever reason, my wife comes to mind, my wife and daughter.

What with the sirens and fire engines, we were awake all night.

"That Book Barn place was like a rat's warren," Helen says.

Oyster is braiding the broken bits of civilization into Mona's hair. The artifacts from my foot, the broken columns and stairways and lightning rods. He's pulled apart her Navajo dream catcher and braids the I Ching coins and glass beads and cords into her hair. The Easter shades of blue and pink feathers.

"We spent the entire evening searching," Helen says. "We checked every book in the children's section. We looked through Science. We checked Religion. We checked Philosophy. Poetry. Folk Stories. We checked Ethnic Literature. We checked all through Fiction."

And Oyster says, "The books were on their computer inventory, but just lost in the store."

So they burned the whole place. For three books. They burned tens of thousands of books to make sure those three were destroyed.

"It seemed our only realistic option," Helen says. "You know what those books can do."

For whatever reason, Sodom and Gomorrah come to mind. How God would spare the city if there was even one good person still in it.

Here's just the opposite. Thousands killed in order to destroy a few.

Imagine a new Dark Age. Imagine the books burning. And the tapes and films and files, the radios and televisions, will all go into the same bonfire.

If we're preventing that world or creating it, I don't know.

It said on the television how two security guards were found dead after the fire.

"Actually," Helen says, "they were dead long before the fire. We needed some time to spread the gasoline."

We're killing people to save lives?

We're burning books to save books?

I ask, what is this trip turning into?

"What it's always been," Oyster says, threading some hair through an I Ching coin. "It's a big power grab."

He says, "You want to keep the world the way it is, Dad, with just you in charge."

Helen, he says, wants the same world, but with her in charge. Every generation wants to be the last. Every generation hates the next trend in music they can't understand. We hate to give up those reins of our culture. To find our own music playing in elevators. The ballad for our revolution, turned into background music for a television commercial. To find our generation's clothes and hair suddenly retro.

"Me," Oyster says, "I'm all for wiping the slate clean, of

books and people, and starting over. I'm for nobody being in charge."

With him and Mona as the new Adam and Eve?

"Nope," he says, smoothing the hair back from Mona's sleeping face. "We'd have to go, too."

I ask, does he hate people so much that he'd kill the woman he loves? I ask, why doesn't he just kill himself?

"No," Oyster says, "I just love everything the same. Plants, animals, humans. I just don't believe the big lie about how we can continue to be fruitful and multiply without destroying ourselves."

I say, he's a traitor to his species.

"I'm a fucking patriot," Oyster says, and looks out his window. "This culling poem is a blessing. Why do you think it was created in the first place? It will save millions of people from the slow terrible death we're headed for from disease, from famine, drought, from solar radiation, from war, from all the places we're headed."

So he's willing to kill himself and Mona? I ask, so what about his parents? Will he just kill them, too? What about all the little children who've had little or no life? What about all the good, hardworking people who live green and recycle? The vegans? Aren't they innocent in his mind?

"This isn't about guilt or innocence," he says. "The dinosaurs weren't morally good or bad, but they're all dead."

That kind of thinking makes him an Adolf Hitler. A Joseph Stalin. A serial killer. A mass murderer.

And threading a stained-glass window into Mona's hair, Oyster says, "I want to be what killed the dinosaurs."

And I say, it was an act of God that killed the dinosaurs.

I say, I'm not going another mile with a wanna-be mass murderer.

And Oyster says, "What about Dr. Sara? Mom? Help me out. How many others has Dad here already killed?"

And Helen says, "I'm sewing my fish."

At the sound of Oyster's cigarette lighter, I turn and ask, does he have to smoke? I say, I'm trying to eat.

But Oyster's got Mona's book about primitive crafts, *Traditional Tribal Hobby-Krafts,* and he's holding it open above the lighter, fanning the pages in the little flame. With his window open a crack, he slips the book out, letting the flames explode in the wind before he drops it.

Cheatgrass loves fire.

He says, "Books can be so evil. Mulberry needs to invent her own kind of spirituality."

Helen's phone rings. Oyster's phone rings.

Mona sighs and stretches her arms. With her eyes closed, Oyster's hands still picking through her hair, his phone still ringing, Mona grinds her head into Oyster's lap and says, "Maybe the grimoire will have a spell to stop overpopulation."

Helen opens the planner book to today's date and writes a name. Into her phone, she says, "Don't bother with an exorcism. We can put the house right back on the market."

Mona says, "You know, we need some kind of universal 'gelding spell.' "

And I ask, isn't anybody here worried about going to hell?

And Oyster takes his phone out of his medicine bag.

His phone ringing and ringing.

Helen puts her phone against her chest and says, "Don't think for a second that the government's not already working on some swell infectious ways to stop overpopulation."

And Oyster says, "In order to save the world, Jesus Christ suffered for about thirty-six hours on the cross." His phone ringing and ringing, he says, "I'm willing to suffer an eternity in hell for the same cause."

His phone ringing and ringing.

Into her phone, Helen says, "Really? Your bedroom smells like sulfur?"

"You figure out who's the better savior," Oyster says, and flips his cell phone open. Into the phone, he says, "Dunbar, Dunaway and Doogan, Attorneys-at-Law . . ."

Chapter 27

Imagine if the Chicago fire of 1871 had gone on for six months before anyone noticed. Imagine if the Johnstown flood in 1889 or the 1906 San Francisco earthquake had lasted six months, a year, two years, before anyone paid attention to it.

Building with wood, building on fault lines, building on floodplains, each era creates its own "natural" disasters.

Imagine a flood of dark green in the downtown of any major city, the office and condo towers submerged inch by inch.

Now, here and now, I'm writing from Seattle. A day, a week, a month late. Who knows how far after the fact. The Sarge and me, we're still witch-hunting.

Hedera helixseattle, botanists are calling this new variety of English ivy. One week, maybe the planters around the Olympic Professional Plaza, they looked a little overgrown. The ivy was *crowding the pansies. Some vines had rooted into the side of the brick facade and were inching up. No one noticed. It had been raining a lot.*

No one noticed until the morning the residents of the Park Senior Living Center found their lobby doors sealed with ivy. That same day, the south wall of the Fremont Theater, brick and concrete three feet thick, it buckled onto a sellout crowd. That same day, part of the underground bus mall caved in.

No one can really say when Hedera helixseattle *first took root, but you can make a good guess.*

Looking through back issues of the Seattle Times, *there's an ad in the May 5 Entertainment section. Three columns wide, it says:*

Attention Patrons of the Oracle Sushi Palace

The ad says, "If you experience severe rectal itching caused by intestinal parasites, you may be eligible to take part in a class-action lawsuit." Then it gives a phone number.

Me, here with the Sarge, I call the number.

A man's voice says, "Denton, Daimler and Dick, Attorneys-at-Law."

And I say, "Oyster?"

I say, "Where are you, you little fuck?"

And the line goes dead.

Here and now, writing this in Seattle, in a diner just outside of the Department of Public Works barricades, a waitress tells the Sarge and me, "They can't kill the ivy now," and she pours us more coffee. She looks out the window at the walls of green, veined with fat gray vines. She says, "It's the only thing holding that part of town together."

Inside the net of vines and leaves, the bricks are buckling and shifted. Cracks shatter the concrete. The windows are squeezed until the glass breaks. Door won't open because the frames are so warped. Birds fly in and out of the straight-up green cliffs, eating the ivy seeds, shitting them everywhere. A block away, the streets are canyons of green, the asphalt and sidewalks buried in green.

"The Green Menace," the newspapers call it. The ivy equivalent of killer bees. The Ivy Inferno.

Silent, unstoppable. The end of civilization in slow motion.

The waitress, she says every time city crews prune the vines, or burn them with flamethrowers, or spray them with poison—even the time they herded in pygmy goats to eat it—the ivy roots spread. The roots collapsed tunnels. They severed underground cables and pipes.

The Sarge dials the number from the sushi ad, again and again, but the line stays dead.

The waitress looks at the fingers of ivy already coming across the street. In another week, she'll be out of a job.

"The National Guard promised us containment," she says.

She says, "I hear they've got the ivy in Portland now, too. And San Francisco." She sighs and says, "We're definitely losing this one."

Chapter 28

The man opens his front door, and here are Helen and I on his front porch, me carrying Helen's cosmetic case, standing a half-step behind her as Helen points the long pink nail of her index finger and says, "Oh God."

She has her daily planner tucked under one arm and says, "My husband," and she steps back. "My husband would like to witness to you about the promise of the Lord Jesus Christ."

Helen's suit is yellow, but not a buttercup yellow. It's more the yellow of a buttercup made of gold and pavé citrons by Carl Fabergé.

The man's holding a bottle of beer. He's wearing gray sweat socks with no shoes. His bathrobe hangs open in the front, and inside, he's wearing a white T-shirt and boxer shorts patterned with little race cars. With one hand, he sticks the beer in his mouth.

His head tips back, and bubbles glub up inside the bottle. The little race cars have oval tires tilted forward. The man belches and says, "You guys for real?"

He has black hair hanging down a wrinkled Frankenstein forehead. He has sad baggy hound-dog eyes.

My hand out front to shake his, I say, Mr. Sierra? I say, we're here to share the joy of God's love.

And the race car guy frowns and says, "How is it you know my name?" He squints at me and says, "Did Bonnie send you to talk to me?"

And Helen leans around him, looking into the living room. She snaps open her purse and takes out a pair of white gloves and starts wiggling her fingers inside. She buttons a little button at the cuff of each glove and says, "May we come in?"

It was supposed to be easier than this.

Plan B, if we find a man at home, we bring out plan B.

The race car guy puts the beer bottle in his mouth, and his stubbly cheeks suck in around it. His head tilts back and the rest of the beer bubbles away. He steps to one side and says, "Well. Sit down." He looks at his empty bottle and says, "Can I get you a beer?"

We step in, and he goes in the kitchen. There's the hiss of him popping a bottle cap.

In the whole living room, there's just a recliner chair. There's a little portable television sitting on a milk crate. Out through sliding glass doors, you can see a patio. Lined up along the far edge of the patio are green florist vases, brimful of rain, rotted black flowers bent and falling out of them. Rotted brown roses on black sticks fuzzy with gray mold. Tied around one arrangement is a wide black satin ribbon.

In the living room shag carpet, there's the ghost outlines left by a sofa. There's the outlines left by a china cabinet, the little dents left by the feet of chairs and tables. There's a big flat square where the carpet is all crushed the same. It looks so familiar.

The race car guy waves me at the recliner and says, "Sit down." He drinks some beer and says, "Sit, and we'll talk about what God's really like."

The big flat square in the carpet, it was left by a playpen.

I ask if my wife can use his bathroom.

And he tilts his head to one side, looking at Helen. With his free hand, he scratches the back of his neck, saying, "Sure. It's at the end of the hall," and he waves with his beer bottle.

Helen looks at the beer sloshed out on the carpet and says, "Thank you." She takes her daily planner from under her arm and hands it to me, saying, "In case you need it, here's a Bible."

Her book full of political targets and real estate closings. Great.

It's still warm from her armpit.

She disappears down the hallway. The sound of a bathroom fan comes on. A door shuts somewhere.

"Sit," the race car guy says.

And I sit.

He stands over me so close I'm afraid to open the daily planner, afraid he'll see it's not a real Bible. He smells like beer and sweat. The little race cars are eye level with me. The oval tires are tilted so they look like they're going fast. The guy takes another drink and says, "Tell me all about God."

The recliner chair smells like him. It's gold velvet, darker brown on the arms from dirt. It's warm. And I say God's a noble, hard-line moralist who refuses to accept anything but steadfast righteous conduct. He's a bastion of upright standards, a lamp that shines its light to reveal the evil of this world. God will always be in our hearts and souls because His own soul is so strong and so un———

"Bullshit," says the guy. He turns away and goes to look out the patio doors. His face is reflected in the glass, just his eyes, with his dark stubbly jaw lost in shadow.

In my best radio preacher voice, I say how God is the moral

yardstick against which millions of people must measure their own lives. He's the flaming sword, sent down to route the misdeeds and evildoers from the temple of——

"Bullshit!" the guy shouts at his reflection in the glass door. Beer spray runs down his reflected face.

Helen is standing in the doorway to the hall, one hand at her mouth, chewing her knuckle. She looks at me and shrugs. She disappears back down the hallway.

From the gold velvet recliner, I say how God is an angel of unparalleled power and impact, a conscience for the world around Him, a world of sin and cruel intent, a world of hidd——

In almost a whisper, the guy says, "Bullshit." The fog of his breath has erased his reflection. He turns to look at me, pointing at me with his beer hand, saying, "Read to me where it says in your Bible something that will fix things."

Helen's daily organizer bound in red leather, I open it a crack and peek inside.

"Tell me how to prove to the police I didn't kill anybody," the guy says.

In the organizer is the name Renny O'Toole and the date June 2. Whoever he is, he's dead. On September 10, Samara Umpirsi is entered. On August 17, Helen closed a deal for a house on Gardner Hill Road. That, and she killed the tyrant king of the Tongle Republic.

"Read!" the race car guy shouts. The beer in his hand foams over his fingers and drips on the carpet. He says, "Read to me where it says I can lose everything in one night and people are going to say it's my fault."

I peek in the book, and it's more names of dead people.

"Read," the guy says, and drinks his beer. "You read where it says a wife can accuse her husband of killing their kid and everybody is supposed to believe her."

Early in the book, the writing is faded and hard to read. The pages are stiff and flyspecked. Before that, someone's started tearing out the oldest pages.

"I asked God," the guy says. He shakes his beer at me and says, "I asked Him to give me a family. I went to church."

I say how maybe God didn't start out by attacking and berating everybody who prayed. I say, maybe it was after years and years of getting the same prayers about unwanted pregnancies, about divorces, about family squabbles. Maybe it was because God's audience grew and more people were making demands. Maybe it was the more praise He got. Maybe power corrupts, but He wasn't always a bastard.

And the race car guy says, "Listen." He says, "I go to court in two days to decide if I'm accused of murder." He says, "You tell me how God is going to save me."

His breath nothing but beer, he says, "You tell me."

Mona would have me tell the truth. To save this guy. To save myself and Helen. To reunite us with humanity. Maybe this guy and his wife would reunite, but then the poem would be out. Millions would die. The rest would live in that world of silence, hearing only what they think is safe. Plugging their ears and burning books, movies, music.

Somewhere a toilet flushes. A bathroom fan shuts off. A door opens.

The guy puts the beer in his mouth and bubbles glug up inside the bottle.

Helen appears in the doorway to the hall.

My foot aches, and I ask, has he considered taking up a hobby? Maybe something he could do in prison.

Constructive destruction. I'm sure Helen would approve of the sacrifice. Condemning one innocent man so millions don't die.

Here's every lab animal who dies to save a dozen cancer patients.

And the race car guy says, "I think you'd better leave."

Walking out to the car, I hand Helen the daily planner and tell her, here's your Bible. My pager goes off, and it's some number I don't know.

Her white gloves are black with dust, and she says she tore up the culling song page and dropped it out the nursery window. It's raining. The paper will rot.

I say, that's not good enough. Some kid could find it. Just the fact that it's tore up will make someone want to put it back together. Some detective investigating the death of a child, maybe.

And Helen says, "That bathroom was a nightmare."

We drive around the block and park. Mona's scribbling in the backseat. Oyster's on his phone. Then Helen waits while I crouch down and walk back to the house. I duck around the back, the wet lawn sucking at my shoes, until I'm under the window Helen says is the nursery. The window's still open, the curtains hanging out a little at the bottom. Pink curtains.

The torn bits of page are scattered in the mud, and I start to pick them all up.

Behind the curtains, in the empty room, you can hear the door open. The outline of somebody comes in from the hallway, and I crouch in the mud under the window. A man's hand comes down on the windowsill so I pull back flat against the house. From somewhere above me where I can't see, a man starts crying.

It starts to rain harder.

The man stands in the window, leaning both hands on the open sill. He sobs louder. You can smell the beer inside him.

Me, I can't run. I can't stand up. With my hands clamped over my nose and mouth, I crouch inches away, squeezed tight against the foundation, hidden. And hitting me as fast as a chill, me breathing between my fingers, I start to cry, too. Sobs as hard as vomiting. My belly cramps. My teeth biting into my palm, the snot sprays into my hands.

The man sniffs, hard and bubbling. It's raining harder, and water seeps into my shoes through the laces.

The torn bits of the poem in my hand, I hold the power of life and death. I just can't do anything. Not yet.

And maybe you don't go to hell for the things you do. Maybe you go to hell for the things you don't do.

My shoes full of cold water, my foot stops hurting. My hand slick with snot and tears, I reach down and turn off my pager.

When we find the grimoire, if there is some way to raise the dead, maybe we won't burn it. Not right away.

Chapter 29

The police report doesn't say how warm my wife, Gina, felt when I woke up that morning. How soft and warm she felt under the covers. How when I turned next to her, she rolled onto her back, her hair fanned out on her pillow. Her head was tipped a little toward one shoulder. Her morning skin smelled warm, the way sunlight looks bouncing up off a white tablecloth in a nice restaurant near the beach on your honeymoon.

Sun came through the blue curtains, making her skin blue. Her lips blue. Her eyelashes were lying across each cheek. Her mouth was a loose smile.

Still half asleep, I cupped my hand behind her neck and tilted her face back and kissed her.

Her neck and shoulder were so easy and relaxed.

Still kissing her warm, relaxed mouth, I pulled her nightgown up around her waist.

Her legs seemed to roll apart, and my hand found her loose and wet inside.

Under the covers, my eyes closed, I worked my tongue inside. With my wet fingers, I peeled back the smooth pink edges of her and licked deeper. The tide of air going in and out of me. At the top of each breath, I drove my mouth up into her.

For once, Katrin had slept the whole night and wasn't crying.

My mouth climbed to Gina's belly button. It climbed to her breasts. With one wet finger in her mouth, my other fingers flick across her nipples. My mouth cups over her other breast and my tongue touches the nipple inside.

Gina's head rolled to one side, and I licked the back of her ear. My hips pressing her legs apart, I put myself inside.

The loose smile on her face, the way her mouth came open at the last moment and her head sunk deep into the pillow, she was so quiet. It was the best it had been since before Katrin was born.

A minute later, I slipped out of bed and took a shower. I tip-toed into my clothes and eased the bedroom door shut behind me. In the nursery, I kissed Katrin on the side of her head. I felt her diaper. The sun came through her yellow curtains. Her toys and books. She looked so perfect.

I felt so blessed.

No one in the world was as lucky as me that morning.

Here, driving Helen's car with her asleep in the front seat beside me. Tonight, we're in Ohio or Iowa or Idaho, with Mona asleep in the back. Helen's pink hair pillowed against my shoulder. Mona sprawled in the rearview mirror, sprawled in her colored pens and books. Oyster asleep. This is the life I have now. For better or for worse. For richer, for poorer.

That was my last really good day. It wasn't until I came home from work that I knew the truth.

Gina was still lying in the same position.

The police report would call it postmortem sexual intercourse. Nash comes to mind.

Katrin was still quiet. The underside of her head had turned dark red.

Livor mortis. Oxygenated hemoglobin.

It wasn't until I came home that I knew what I'd done.

Here, parked in the leather smell of Helen's big Realtor car, the sun is just above the horizon. It's the same moment now as it was then. We're parked under a tree, on a treelined street in a neighborhood of little houses. It's some kind of flowering tree, and all night, pink flower petals have fallen on the car, sticking to the dew. Helen's car is pink as a parade float, covered in flowers, and I'm spying out through just a hole where the petals don't cover the windshield.

The morning light shining in through the layer of petals is pink.

Rose-colored. On Helen and Mona and Oyster, asleep.

Down the block, an old couple is working in the flower beds along their foundation. The old man fills a watering can at a spigot. The old woman kneels, pulling weeds.

I turn my pager back on, and it starts beeping right away.

Helen jerks awake.

The phone number on my pager, I don't recognize it.

Helen sits up, blinking, looking at me. She looks at the tiny sparkling watch on her wrist. On one side of her face are deep red pockmarks where she slept on her dangling emerald earrings. She looks at the layer of pink covering all the windows. She plunges the pink fingernails of both hands into her hair and fluffs it, saying, "Where are we now?"

Some people still think knowledge is power.

I tell her, I have no idea.

Chapter 30

Mona stands at my elbow. She holds a glossy brochure open, pushing it in my face, saying, "Can we go here? Please? Just for a couple hours? Please?"

Photographs in the brochure show people screaming with their hands in the air, riding a roller coaster. Photos show people driving go-carts around a track outlined in old tires. More people are eating cotton candy and riding plastic horses on a merry-go-round. Other people are locked into seats on a Ferris wheel. Along the top of the brochure in big scrolling letters it says: *LaughLand, The Family Place.*

Except in place of the *a*'s are four laughing clown faces. A mother, a father, a son, a daughter.

We have another eighty-four books to disarm. That's dozens more libraries in cities all over the country. Then there's the grimoire to find. There's people to bring back from the dead. Or just castrate. Or there's all of humanity to kill, depending on whom you ask.

There's so much we need to get fixed. To get back to God, as Mona would say. Just to break even.

Karl Marx would say we've made every plant and animal our enemy to justify killing it.

In the newspaper today, it says the husband of one of the fashion models is being held under suspicion of murder.

I'm standing at a public phone outside some small-town library while Helen's inside trashing another book with Oyster.

A man's voice on the phone says, "Homicide Division."

Into the phone, I ask, who is this?

And the voice says, "Detective Ben Danton, Homicide Division." He says, "Who is this?"

A police detective. Mona would call him my savior, sent to wrangle me back into the fold with the rest of humanity. This is the number that's been appearing on my pager for the past couple days.

Mona turns the brochure over and says, "Just look." Braided in her hair are broken windmills and train trestles and radio towers.

Photos show smiling children getting hugged by clowns. It shows parents strolling hand in hand and riding little skiffs through a Tunnel of Love.

She says, "This trip doesn't have to be all work."

Helen comes out of the library doors and starts down the front steps, and Mona turns and rushes at her, saying, "Helen, Mr. Streator said it was okay."

And I put the pay phone receiver to my chest and say, I did not.

Oyster is hanging back, a step behind Helen's elbow.

Mona holds the brochure in Helen's face, saying, "Look how much fun."

On the phone, Detective Danton says, "Who is this?"

It was okay to sacrifice the poor guy in his race car boxer

shorts. It's okay to sacrifice the young woman in the apron printed with little chickens. To not tell them the truth, to let them suffer. And to sacrifice the widower of some fashion model. But sacrificing me to save the millions is another thing altogether.

Into the phone, I say my name, Streator, and that he paged me.

"Mr. Streator," he says, "we'd like you to come in for questioning."

I ask, about what?

"Why don't we talk about that in person?" he says.

I ask if this is about a death.

"When can you make it in?" he says.

I ask if this is about the series of deaths with no apparent cause.

"Sooner would be better than later," he says.

I ask if this is because one victim was my upstairs neighbor and three were my editors.

And Danton says, "You don't say?"

I ask if this is because I passed three more victims in the street the moment before they each died.

And Danton says, "That's news to me."

I ask if this is because I stood within spitting distance of the young sideburns guy who died in the bar on Third Avenue.

"Uh-huh," he says. "You'd mean Marty Latanzi."

I ask if this is because all the dead fashion models show signs of postmortem sex, the same way my wife did twenty years ago. And no doubt they have security camera film of me talking to a librarian named Symon at the moment he dropped dead.

You can hear a pencil somewhere scratching fast notes on paper.

Away from the phone, I hear someone else say, "Keep him on the line."

I ask if this is really a ploy to arrest me for suspicion of murder.

And Detective Danton says, "Don't make us issue a bench warrant."

The more people die, the more things stay the same.

Officer Danton, I say. I ask, can he tell me where to find him at this exact moment?

Sticks and stones may break your bones, but here we go again. Fast as a scream, the culling song spins through my head, and the phone line goes dead.

I've killed my savior. Detective Ben Danton. I'm that much further from the rest of humanity.

Constructive destruction.

Oyster shakes his plastic cigarette lighter, slapping it against the palm of one hand. Then he gives it to Helen and watches while she takes a folded page out of her purse. She lights the page 27 and holds it over the gutter.

While Mona's reading the brochure, Helen holds the burning page near the edge of it. The photos of happy, smiling families puff into flame, and Mona shrieks and drops them. Still holding the burning page, Helen kicks the burning families into the gutter. The fire in her hand gets bigger and bigger, stuttering and smoking in the breeze.

And for whatever reason, I think of Nash and his burning fuse.

Helen says, "I don't do *fun*." With her other hand, Helen jingles her car keys at me.

Then it happens. Oyster has his arm locked around Helen's head from behind. That fast, he knocks her off her feet and as she throws her arms out for balance, he grabs the burning poem. The culling song.

Helen drops to her knees, drops out of his grip, she cries just one little scream when her knees hit the concrete sidewalk, and she tumbles into the gutter. Her keys still in her fist.

Oyster beats the burning page against his thigh. He holds it in both hands, his eyes twitching back and forth, reading down the page as the fire rolls up from the bottom.

Both his hands are on fire before he lets go, yelling, "No!" and sticks his fingers into his mouth.

Mona steps back, her hands pressed over her ears. Her eyes squeezed shut.

Helen on her hands and knees in the gutter, next to the burning families, she looks up at Oyster. Oyster as good as dead. Helen's hairdo is broken open and pink hair hangs in her eyes. Her nylons are torn. Her knees, bloody.

"Don't kill him!" Mona yells. "Don't kill him, please! Don't kill him!"

Oyster drops to his knees and grabs at the burned paper on the sidewalk.

And slow, slow as the hour hand on a clock, Helen rises to her feet. Her face is red. It's not the red of a Burmese ruby. It's more the red of the blood running down from her knees.

With Oyster kneeling. With Helen standing over him. With Mona holding both hands over her ears, squeezing her eyes shut. Oyster's sifting through his ashes. Helen's bleeding. Me, I'm still watching from the phone booth, and a flock of starlings flies up from the roof of the library.

Oyster, the evil, resentful, violent son Helen might have, if she still had a son.

Just the same old power grab.

"Go ahead," Oyster says, and he lifts his head to meet Helen's eyes. He smiles with just half his mouth and says, "You killed your real son. You can kill me."

And then it happens. Helen slaps him hard across the face, dragging her fistful of keys through each cheek. A moment later, more blood.

Another scarred parasite. Another mutilated cockroach armoire.

And Helen's eyes snap up from Oyster bleeding to the starlings circling above us, and bird by bird, they drop. Their black feathers flashing an oily blue. Their dead eyes just staring black beads. Oyster holds his face, both his hands full of blood. Helen glaring up into the sky, the shining black bodies hiss down and bounce, bird by bird, around us on the concrete.

Constructive destruction.

Chapter 31

A mile outside of town, Helen pulls over to the side of the highway. She puts on the car's emergency flashers. Looking at nothing but her hands, her skintight calfskin driving gloves on the steering wheel, she says, "Get out."

On the windshield, there are little contact lenses of water. It's starting to rain.

"Fine," Oyster says, and jerks his car door open. He says, "Isn't this what people do with dogs they can't house-train?"

His face and hands are smeared red with blood. The devil's face. His shattered blond hair sticks up from his forehead, stiff and red as devil's horns. His red goatee. In all this red, his eyes are white. It's not the white of white flags, surrender. It's the white of hard-boiled eggs, crippled chickens in battery cages, factory farm misery and suffering and death.

"Just like Adam and Eve getting evicted from the Garden of Eden," he says. Oyster stands on the gravel shoulder of the highway and leans down to look at Mona still in the backseat, and he says, "You coming, Eve?"

It's not about love, it's about control.

Behind Oyster, the sun's going down. Behind him is Russian thistle and Scotch broom and kudzu. Behind him, the whole world's a mess.

And Mona with the ruins of Western civilization braided into her hair, the bits of dream catcher and I Ching, she looks at her black fingernails in her lap and says, "Oyster, what you did is wrong."

Oyster puts his hand into the car, reaching across the seat to her, his hand red and clotted, and he says, "Mulberry, despite all your herbal good intentions, this trip is not going to work." He says, "Come with me."

Mona sets her teeth together and snaps her face to look at him, saying, "You threw away my Indian crafts book." She says, "That book was very important to me."

Some people still think knowledge is power.

"Mulberry, honey," Oyster says, and strokes her hair, the hair sticking to his bloody hand. He tucks a skein of hair behind her ear and says, "That book was fucked."

"Fine," says Mona, and she pulls away and folds her arms.

And Oyster says, "Fine." And he slams the car door, his hand leaving a bloody print on the window.

His red hands raised at his sides, Oyster steps back from the car. Shaking his head, he says, "Forget about me. I'm just another one of God's alligators you can flush down the toilet."

Helen shifts the car into drive. She touches some switch, and Oyster's door locks.

And from outside the locked car, muffled and fuzzy, Oyster yells, "You can flush me, but I'll just keep eating shit." He shouts, "And I'll just keep growing."

Helen puts on her turn signal and starts out into traffic.

"You can forget me," Oyster yells. With his red yelling devil face, his teeth big and white, he yells, "But that doesn't mean I don't still exist."

For whatever reason, the first gypsy moth that flew out a window in Medford, Massachusetts, in 1860 comes to mind.

And driving, Helen touches her eye with one finger, and when she puts her hand back on the steering wheel, the glove finger is a darker brown. Wet. And for better or for worse. For richer or poorer. This is her life.

Mona puts her face in both hands and starts to sob.

And counting 1, counting 2, counting 3 . . . , I turn on the radio.

Chapter 32

The town's name is Stone River on the map. Stone River, Nebraska. But when the Sarge and I get there, the sign at the city limits is painted over with the name "Shivapuram."

Nebraska.

Population 17,000.

In the middle of the street, straddling the center line dashes is a brown and white cow we have to swerve around. Chewing its cud, the cow doesn't flinch.

The downtown is two blocks of red-brick buildings. A yellow signal light blinks above the main intersection. A black cow is scratching its side against the metal pole of a stop sign. A white cow eats zinnias out of a window box in front of the post office. Another cow lies, blocking the sidewalk in front of the police station.

You smell curry and patchouli. The deputy sheriff's wearing

sandals. The deputy, the mailman, the waitress in the café, the bar-tender in the tavern, they're all wearing a black dot pasted between their eyes. A bindi.

"Crimony," the Sarge says. "The whole town's gone Hindu."

According to this week's Psychic Wonders Bulletin, *this is all because of the talking Judas Cow.*

In any slaughterhouse operation, the trick is to fool cows into climbing the chute that leads to the killing floor. Cows trucked in from farms, they're confused, scared. After hours or days squeezed into trucks, dehydrated and awake the whole trip, the cows are thrown in with other cows in the feedlot outside the slaughterhouse.

How you get them to climb the chute is you send in the Judas Cow. This is really what this cow is called. It's a cow that lives at the slaughterhouse. It mingles with the doomed cows, then leads them up the chute to the killing floor. The scared, spooked cows would never go except for the Judas Cow leading the way.

The last step before the ax or the knife or the steel bolt through the skull, at that last moment, the Judas Cow steps aside. It survives to lead another herd to their death. It does this for its entire life.

Until, according to the Psychic Wonders Bulletin, *the Judas Cow at the Stone River Meatpacking Plant, one day it stopped.*

The Judas Cow stood blocking the doorway to the killing floor. It refused to step aside and let the herd behind it die. With the whole slaughterhouse crew watching, the Judas Cow sat on its hind legs, the way a dog sits, the cow sat there in the doorway and looked at everyone with its brown cow eyes and talked.

The Judas Cow talked.

It said, "Reject your meat-eating ways."

The cow's voice was the voice of a young woman. The cows in line behind it, they shifted their weight from foot to foot, waiting.

The slaughterhouse crew, their mouths fell open so fast their cig-arettes dropped out on the bloody floor. One man swallowed his chewing tobacco. A woman screamed through her fingers.

The Judas Cow, sitting there, it raised one front leg to point its hoof at the crew and said, "The path to moksha is not through the pain and suffering of other creatures."

"Moksha" says the Psychic Wonders Bulletin, is a Sanskrit word for "redemption," the end of the karmic cycle of reincarnation.

The Judas Cow talked all afternoon. It said human beings had destroyed the natural world. It said mankind must stop exterminating other species. Man must limit his numbers, create a quota system which allows only a small percentage of the planet's beings to be human. Humans could live any way they liked so long as they were not the majority.

It taught them a Hindi song. The cow made the whole crew sing along while it swung its hoof back and forth to the beat of the song.

The cow answered all their questions about the nature of life and death.

The Judas Cow just droned on and on and on.

Now, here and now, the Sarge and I, we're here after the fact. Witch-hunting. We're looking at all the cows released from the meatpacking plant that day. The plant is empty and quiet on the far edge of town. Someone's painting the concrete building pink. Making it into an ashram. They've planted vegetables in the feedlot.

The Judas Cow hasn't said a word since. It eats the grass in people's front yards. It drinks from birdbaths. People hang daisy chains around its neck.

"They're using the occupation spell," the Sarge says. We're stopped in the street, waiting for a huge slow hog to cross in front of our car. Other pigs and chickens stand in the shade under the hardware store awning.

An occupation spell lets you project your consciousness into the physical body of another being.

I look at him, too long, and ask if he isn't the pot calling the kettle black.

"Animals, people," the Sarge says, "you can put yourself into pretty much any living body."

And I say, yeah, tell me about it.

We drive past the man painting the pink ashram, and the Sarge says, "If you ask me, reincarnation is just another way to procrastinate."

And I say, yeah, yeah, yeah. He's already told me that one.

The Sarge reaches across the front seat to put his wrinkled spotted hand over mine. The back of his hand is carpeted with gray hairs. His fingers are cold from handling his pistol. The Sarge squeezes my hand and says, "Do you still love me?"

And I ask if I have a choice.

Chapter 33

The crowds of people shoulder around us, the women in halter tops and men in cowboy hats. People are eating caramel apples on sticks and shaved ice in paper cones. Dust is everywhere. Somebody steps on Helen's foot and she pulls it back, saying, "I find that no matter how many people I kill, it's never enough."

I say, let's not talk shop.

The ground is crisscrossed with thick black cables. In the darkness beyond the lights, engines burn diesel to make electricity. You can smell diesel and deep-fried food and vomit and powdered sugar.

These days, this is what passes for fun.

A scream sails past us. And a glimpse of Mona. It's a carnival ride with a bright neon sign that says: *The Octopus*. Black metal arms, like twisted spokes, turn around a hub. At the same time, they dip up and down. At the end of each arm is a seat, and each seat spins on its own hub. The scream sails by again, and a banner of red and black hair. Her silver chains and charms are flung straight out from the side of Mona's neck. Both her hands are clamped on the guard bar fastened across her lap.

The ruins of Western civilization, the turrets and towers and chimneys, fly out of Mona's hair. An I Ching coin bullets past us.

Helen watches her, saying, "I guess Mona got her flying spell."

My pager goes off again. It's the same number as the police detective. A new savior is already hot on my tail.

The more people die, the more things stay the same.

I turn the pager off.

And watching Mona scream by, Helen says, "Bad news?"

I say, nothing important.

In her pink high heels, Helen picks through the mud and saw-dust, stepping over the black power cables.

Holding out my hand, I say, "Here."

And she takes it. And I don't let go. And she doesn't seem to mind. And we're walking hand in hand. And it's nice.

She's only got a few big rings left so it doesn't hurt as much as you'd think.

The carnival rides thrash the air around us, diamond-white, emerald-green, ruby-red lights, turquoise and sapphire-blue lights, the yellow of citrons, the orange of honey amber. Rock music blares out of speakers mounted on poles everywhere.

These rock-oholics. These quiet-ophobics.

I ask Helen, when was the last time she rode a Ferris wheel?

Everywhere, there are men and women, hand in hand, kissing. They're feeding each other shreds of pink cotton candy. They walk side by side, each with one hand stuck in the butt pocket of the other's tight jeans.

Watching the crowd, Helen says, "Don't take this the wrong way, but when was your last time?"

My last time for what?

"You know."

I'm not sure if my last time counts, but it must be about eighteen years ago.

And Helen smiles and says, "It's no wonder you walk funny." She says, "I have twenty years and counting since John."

On the ground, with the sawdust and cables, there's a crumbled newspaper page. A three-column advertisement says:

Attention Patrons of the Helen Boyle Real Estate Agency

The ad says, "Have you been sold a haunted house? If so, please call the following number to be part of a class-action lawsuit."

Then Oyster's cell phone number. Then I say, please, Helen, why did you tell him that stuff?

Helen looks down at the newspaper ad. With her pink shoe, she grinds it into the mud, saying, "For the same reason I didn't kill him. He could be very lovable at times."

Next to the ad, covered in mud is the photo of another dead fashion model.

Looking up at the Ferris wheel, a ring of red and white fluorescent tubes holding seats that sway full of people, Helen says, "That looks doable."

A man stops the wheel and all the carts swing in place while Helen and I sit on the red plastic cushion and the man snaps a guard bar shut across our laps. He steps back and pulls a lever, and the big diesel engine catches. The Ferris wheel jerks as if it's rolling backward, and Helen and I rise into the darkness.

Halfway up into the night, the wheel jerks to a stop. Our seat swings, and Helen makes a fast grab for the guard bar. A diamond solitaire slips off one finger and flashes straight through the struts and lights, through the colors and faces, down into the gears of the machine.

Helen looks after it, saying, "Well, that was roughly thirty-five thousand dollars."

I say, maybe it's okay. It's a diamond.

And Helen says that's the problem. Gemstones are the hardest things on earth, but they still break. They can take constant stress and pressure, but a sudden, sharp impact can shatter them into dust.

Across the midway floor, Mona comes running over the sawdust to stand below us, waving both hands. She jumps in place and yells, "Whooooo! Go, Helen!"

The wheel jerks, starting again. The seat tilts, and Helen's purse starts to fall but she grabs it. The gray rock's still inside it. The gift from Oyster's coven. Instead of her purse, her planner book slides off the seat, flapping open in the air, tumbling down to land in the sawdust, and Mona runs over and picks it up.

Mona slaps the book on her thigh to knock off the sawdust, then shakes it in the air to show it's okay.

Helen says, "Thank God for Mona."

I say, Mona said you planned to kill me.

And Helen says, "She told me that you wanted to kill me."

We both look at each other.

I say, thank God for Mona.

And Helen says, "Buy me some caramel corn?"

On the ground, farther and farther away, Mona's looking through the pages of the planner. Every day, the name of Helen's political target.

Looking up, out of the colored lights and into the night sky, we're getting closer to the stars. Mona once said that stars are the best part of being alive. On the other side, where people go after they die, they can't see the stars.

Think of deep outer space, the incredible cold and quiet. The heaven where silence is reward enough.

I tell Helen that I need to go home and clean something up. It has to be pretty soon, before things get worse.

The dead fashion models. Nash. The police detectives. All of it. How he got the culling spell, I don't know.

We rise higher, farther away from the smells, away from the diesel engine noise. We rise up into the quiet and cold. Mona, reading the planner book, gets smaller. All the crowds of people, their money and elbows and cowboy boots, get smaller. The food booths and the portable toilets get smaller. The screams and rock music, smaller.

At the top, we jerk to a stop. Our seat sways less and less until we're sitting still. This high up, the breeze teases, rats, back-combs Helen's pink bubble of hair. The neon and grease and mud, from this far away it all looks perfect. Perfect, safe, and happy. The music's just a dull thud, thud, thud.

This is how we must look to God.

Looking down at the rides, the spinning colors and screams, Helen says, "I'm glad you found me out. I think I always hoped someone would." She says, "I'm glad it was you."

Her life isn't so bad, I say. She has her jewels. She has Patrick.

"Still," she says, "it's nice to have one person who knows all your secrets."

Her suit is light blue, but it's not a regular robin's-egg blue. It's the blue of a robin's egg you might find and then worry that it won't hatch because it's dead inside. And then it *does hatch*, and you worry about what to do next.

On the guard bar locked across us, Helen puts her hand on mine and says, "Mr. Streator, do you even *have* a first name?"

Carl.

I say, Carl. It's Carl Streator.

I ask, why did she call me middle-aged?

And Helen laughs and says, "Because you are. We both are."

The wheel jerks again, and we're coming back down.

And I say, her eyes. I say, they're blue.

And this is my life.

At the bottom, the carnival man snaps open the guard bar and

I give Helen my hand as she steps out of the seat. The sawdust is loose and soft, and we limp and stumble through the crowds, holding each other around the waist. We get to Mona, and she's still reading the planner book.

"Time for some caramel corn," Helen says. "Carl, here, is going to buy."

And the book still open in her hands, Mona looks up. Her mouth open a little, her eyes blink once, twice, three times, fast. She sighs and says, "You know the grimoire we're looking for?" She says, "I think we just found it."

Chapter 34

Some witches write their spells in runes, secret coded symbols. According to Mona, some witches write backward so the spell can only be read in a mirror. They write spells in spirals, starting in the center of the page and curving outward. Some write like the ancient Greek curse tablets with one line running from left to right, then the next running right to left and the next, left to right. This, they call the *boustrophedon* form because it mimics the back-and-forth pacing of an ox tied to a tether. To mimic a snake, Mona says, some write each line so it branches in a different direction.

The only rule was, a spell has to be twisted. The more hidden, the more twisted, the more powerful the spell. To witches, the twists themselves are magical. They draw or sculpt the magician-god Hephaestus with his legs twisted.

The more twisted the spell, the more it will twist and hobble the victim. It'll confuse them. Occupy their attention. They'll stumble. Get dizzy. Not concentrate.

The same as Big Brother with all his singing and dancing.

In the gravel parking lot, halfway between the carnival and Helen's car, Mona holds the daily planner book so the lights of the carnival shine through just one page. At first, the only things there are the notes Helen's written for that day. The name "Captain Antonio Cappelle," and a list of real estate appointments. Then you can see a faint pattern in the paper, red words, yellow sentences, blue paragraphs, as each colored light passes behind the page.

"Invisible ink," Mona says, still holding the page out.

It's faint as a watermark, ghostwriting.

"What tipped me off is the binding," Mona says.

The cover and binding are dark red leather, polished almost black with handling.

"It's human skin," Mona says.

It was in Basil Frankie's house, Helen says. It looked like a lovely old book, an empty book. She bought it with Frankie's estate. On the cover is a black five-pointed star.

"A pentagram," Mona says. "And before it was a book, this was somebody's tattoo. This little bump," she says, touching a spot on the book's spine, "this is a nipple."

Mona closes the book and holds it out to Helen and says, "Feel." She says, "This is beyond ancient."

And Helen snaps her purse open and gets out her pair of little white gloves with a button at the cuff. She says, "No, you hold it."

Looking at the book, open in her hands, Mona leafs back and forth. She says, "If I just knew what they used as ink, I'd know how to read it."

If it's ammonia or vinegar, she says, you'd boil a red cabbage and daub on some of the broth to turn the ink purple.

If it's semen, you could read it under fluorescent light.

I say, people wrote spells in peter tracks?

And Mona says, "Only the most powerful type of spells."

If it's written in a clear solution of cornstarch, she could daub on iodine to make the letters stand out.

If it was lemon juice, she says, you'd heat the pages to make the ink turn brown.

"Try tasting it," Helen says, "to see if it's sour."

And Mona slams the book shut. "It's a thousand-year-old witch book bound in mummified skin and probably written in ancient cum." She says to Helen, *"You lick it."*

And Helen says, "Okay, I get your point. Try at least to hurry and translate it."

And Mona says, "I'm not the one who's been carrying it around for ten years. I'm not the one who's been ruining it, writing over the top of everything." She holds the book in both hands and shoves it at Helen. "This is an ancient book. It's written in archaic forms of Greek and Latin, plus some forgotten kinds of runes." She says, "I'm going to need some time."

"Here," Helen says, and snaps open her purse. She takes out a folded square of paper and hands it to Mona, saying, "Here's a copy of the culling song. A man named Basil Frankie translated this much. If you can match it to one of the spells in that book, you can use that as a key to translate all the spells in that language." She says, "Like in the Rosetta stone."

And Mona reaches to take the folded paper.

And I snatch it from Helen's hand and ask, why are we even having this discussion? I say, my idea was we'd burn the book. I open the paper, and it's a page 27 stolen from some library, and I say, we need to think about this.

To Helen, I say, are you sure you want to do this to Mona? This spell has pretty much ruined our lives. I say, besides, what Mona knows, Oyster is going to know.

Helen is flexing her fingers into the white gloves. She buttons each cuff and reaches out to Mona, saying, "Give me the book."

"I can do it," Mona says.

Helen shakes her hand at Mona and says, "No, this is best. Mr. Streator's right. It will change things for you."

The night air is full of faint faraway screams and glowing colors.

And Mona says, "No," and wraps both arms around the book, holding it to her chest.

"You see," Helen says. "It's already started. When there's the possibility of a little power, you already want more."

I tell her to give the book to Helen.

And Mona turns her back to us, saying, "I'm the one who found it. I'm the only one who can read it." She turns to look over one shoulder at me and says, "You, you just want to destroy it so you can sell the story. You want everything resolved so it's safe to talk about."

And Helen says, "Mona, honey, don't."

And Mona turns to look over her other shoulder at Helen and says, "You just want it so you can rule the world. You're just into the money side of everything." Her shoulders roll forward until she seems to wrap her whole body around the book, and she looks down on it, saying, "I'm the only one who appreciates it for what it is."

And I tell her, listen to Helen.

"It's a Book of Shadows," Mona says, "a *real* Book of Shadows. It belongs with a real witch. Just let me translate it. I'll tell you what I find. I promise."

Me, I fold the culling spell from Helen and tuck it in my back pocket. I take a step closer to Mona. I look at Helen, and she nods.

Still with her back to us, Mona says, "I'll bring Patrick back." She says, "I'll bring back all the little children."

And I grab her around the waist from behind and lift. Mona's screaming, kicking her heels into my shins and twisting from side to side, still holding the book, and I work my hands up under her arms until I'm touching it, touching dead human skin. The dead nipple. Mona's nipples. Mona's screaming, and her fingernails dig into my hands, the soft skin between my fingers. She digs into the skin on the back of my hands until I get her around the wrists and twist her arms up and away from her sides. The book falls, and her kicking legs knock it away, and in the dark parking lot, with the distant screams, nobody notices.

This is the life I got. This is the daughter I knew I'd lose someday. Over a boyfriend. Over bad grades. Drugs. Somehow this break always happens. This power struggle. No matter how great a father you think you'll make, at some time you'll find yourself here.

There are worse things you can do to the people you love than kill them.

The book lands in a spray of dust and gravel.

And I yell for Helen to get it.

The moment Mona is free, Helen and I step back. Helen holding the book, I'm looking to see if anybody's around.

Her hands in fists, Mona leans toward us, her red and black hair hanging in her face. Her silver chains and charms are tangled in her hair. Her orange dress is twisted tight around her body, the neckline torn on one side so her shoulder shows, bare. She's kicked off her sandals so she's barefoot. Her eyes behind the dark snarls of her hair, her eyes reflecting the carnival lights, the screams in the distance could be the echo of her screams going on and on, forever.

How she looks is wicked. A wicked witch. A sorceress. Twisted. She's no longer my daughter. Now she's someone I may never understand. A stranger.

And through her teeth, she says, "I could kill you. I could."

And I finger-comb my hair. I straighten my tie and tuck the front of my shirt smooth. I'm counting 1, counting 2, counting 3, and I tell her, no, but we could kill her. I tell her she owes Mrs. Boyle an apology.

This is what passes as tough love.

Helen stands, holding the book in her white-gloved hands, looking at Mona.

Mona says nothing.

The smoke from the diesel generators, the screams and rock music and colored lights, do their best to fill the silence. The stars in the night sky don't say a word.

Helen turns to me and says, "I'm okay. Let's just get going." She gets out her car keys and gives them to me. Helen and I, we turn away and start walking. But looking back, I see Mona laughing into her hands.

She's laughing.

Mona stops laughing when I see, but her smile is still there.

And I tell her to wipe the smirk off her face. I ask, what the hell does she have to smirk about?

Chapter 35

With me driving, Mona sits in the backseat with her arms folded. Helen sits in the front seat next to me, the grimoire open in her lap, lifting each page against her window so she can see sunlight through it. On the front seat between us, her cell phone rings.

At home, Helen says, she still has all the reference books from Basil Frankie's estate. These include translation dictionaries for Greek, Latin, Sanskrit. There are books on ancient cuneiform writing. All the dead languages. Something in one of these books will let her translate the grimoire. Using the culling spell as a sort of code key, a Rosetta stone, she might be able to translate them all.

And Helen's cell phone rings.

In the rearview mirror, Mona picks her nose and rolls the

booger against the leg of her jeans until it's a hard dark lump. She looks up from her lap, her eyes rolling up, slow, until she's looking at the back of Helen's head.

Helen's cell phone rings.

And Mona flicks her booger into the back of Helen's pink hair.

And Helen's cell phone rings. Her eyes still in the grimoire, Helen pushes the phone across the seat until it presses my thigh, saying, "Tell them I'm busy."

It could be the State Department with her next hit assignment. It could be some other government, some cloak-and-dagger business to conduct. A drug kingpin to rub out. Or a career criminal to retire.

Mona opens her green brocade Mirror Book, her witch's diary, in her lap and starts scribbling in it with colored pens.

On the phone is a woman.

It's a client of hers, I tell Helen. Holding the phone against my chest, I say, the woman says a severed head bounced down her front stairway last night.

Still reading the grimoire, Helen says, "That would be the five-bedroom Dutch Colonial on Feeney Drive." She says, "Did it disappear before it landed in the foyer?"

I ask.

To Helen, I say, yes, it disappeared about halfway down the stairway. A hideous bloody head with a leering smile.

The woman on the phone says something.

And broken teeth, I say. She sounds very upset.

Mona's scribbling so hard the colored pens squeak against the paper.

And still reading the grimoire, Helen says, "It disappeared. End of problem."

The woman on the phone says, it happens every night.

"So call an exterminator," Helen says. She holds another page against the sunlight and says, "Tell her I'm not here."

The picture that Mona's drawing in her Mirror Book, it's a

man and woman being struck by lightning, then being run over by a tank, then bleeding to death through their eyes. Their brains spray out their ears. The woman wears a tailored suit and a lot of jewelry. The man, a blue tie.

I'm counting 1, counting 2, counting 3 . . .

Mona takes the man and woman and tears them into thin strips.

The phone rings again, and I answer it.

I hold the phone against my chest and tell Helen, it's some guy. He says his shower sprays blood.

Still holding the grimoire against the window, Helen says, "The six-bedroom on Pender Court."

And Mona says, "Pender *Place*. Pender Court has the severed hand that crawls out of the garbage disposal." She opens the car window a little and starts feeding the shredded man and woman out through the crack.

"You're thinking of the severed hand at Palm Corners," Helen says. "Pender Place has the biting phantom Doberman."

The man on the phone, I ask him to please hold. I press the red HOLD button.

Mona rolls her eyes and says, "The biting ghost is in the Spanish house just off Millstone Boulevard." She starts writing something with a red felt-tip pen, writing so the words spiral out from the center of the page.

I'm counting 9, counting 10, counting 11 . . .

Squinting at the lines of faint writing on the page she has spread against the window, Helen says, "Tell them I'm out of the real estate business." Trailing her finger along under each faint word, she says, "The people at Pender Court, they have teenagers, right?"

I ask, and the man on the phone says yes.

And Helen turns to look at Mona in the backseat, Mona flicking another rolled booger, and Helen says, "Then tell him a bathtub full of human blood is the least of his problems."

I say, how about we just keep driving? We could hit a few more libraries. See some sights. Another carnival, maybe. A national monument. We could have some laughs, loosen up a little. We were a family once, we could be one again. We still love each other, hypothetically speaking. I say, how about it?

Mona leans forward and yanks a few strands of hair out of my head. She leans and yanks a few pink strands from Helen.

And Helen ducks forward over the grimoire, saying, "Mona, that hurt."

In my family, I say, my parents and I, we could settle almost any squabble over a rousing game of Parcheesi.

The strands of pink and brown hair, Mona folds them inside the page of spiral writing.

And I tell Mona, I just don't want her to make the same mistakes I made. Looking at her in the rearview mirror, I say, when I was about her age, I stopped talking to my parents. I haven't talked to them in almost twenty years.

And Mona sticks a baby pin through the page folded with our hair inside.

Helen's phone rings again, and this time it's a man. A young man.

It's Oyster. And before I can hang up, he says, "Hey, Dad, you'll want to make sure and read tomorrow's newspaper." He says, "I put a little surprise in it for you."

He says, "Now, let me talk to Mulberry."

I say her name's Mona. Mona Sabbat.

"It's Mona Steinner," Helen says, still holding a page of the grimoire to the window, trying to read the secret writing.

And Mona says, "Is that Oyster?" From the backseat, she reaches around both sides of my head, grabbing for the phone and saying, "Let me talk." She shouts, "Oyster! Oyster, they have the grimoire!"

And me trying to steer the car, the car veering all over the highway, I flip the phone shut.

Chapter 36

Instead of the stain on my apartment ceiling, there's a big patch of white. Pushpinned to my front door, there's a note from the landlord. Instead of noise, there's total quiet. The carpet is crunchy with little bits of plastic, broken-down doors and flying buttresses. You can hear the filament buzzing in each lightbulb. You can hear my watch tick.

In my refrigerator, the milk's gone sour. All that pain and suffering wasted. The cheese is huge and blue with mold. A package of hamburger has gone gray inside its plastic wrap. The eggs look okay, but they're not, they can't be, not after this long. All the effort and misery that went into this food, and it's all going in the garbage. The contributions of all those miserable cows and veals, it gets thrown out.

The note from my landlord says the white patch on the ceiling is a primer coat. It says when the stain stops bleeding through, they'll paint the whole ceiling. The heat's on high to dry the primer faster. Half the water in the toilet's evaporated. The plants are dry as paper. The trap under the kitchen sink's half empty and sewer gas is leaking back up. My old way of life, everything I call home, smells of shit.

The primer coat is to keep what was left of my upstairs neighbor from bleeding through.

Out in the world, there's still thirty-nine copies of the poems book unaccounted for. In libraries, in bookstores, in homes. Give or take, I don't know, a few dozen.

Helen's in her office today. That's where I left her, sitting at her desk with dictionaries open around her, Greek, Latin, and Sanskrit dictionaries, translation dictionaries. She's got a little bottle of iodine and she's using a cotton swab to daub it on the writing, turning the invisible words red.

Using cotton swabs, Helen's daubing the juice from a purple cabbage on other invisible words, turning them purple.

Next to the little bottles and cotton swabs and dictionaries sits a light with a handle. A cord trails from it to an outlet in the wall.

"A fluoroscope," Helen says. "It's rented." She flicks a switch on the side and holds the light over the open grimoire, turning the pages until one page is filled with glowing pink words. "This one's written in semen."

On all the spells, the handwriting's different.

Mona, at her desk in the outer office, hasn't said a nice word since the carnival. The police scanner is saying one emergency code after another.

Helen calls to Mona, "What's a good word for 'demon'?"

And Mona says, "Helen Hoover Boyle."

Helen looks at me and says, "Have you seen today's paper?" She shoves some books to one side, and under them is a newspaper. She flips through it, and there on the back page of the first section is a full-page ad. The first line says:

Attention, Have You Seen This Man?

Most of the page is an old picture, my wedding picture, me and Gina smiling twenty years ago. This has to be from our wedding announcement in some ancient Saturday edition. Our public declaration of commitment and love for each other. Our pledge. Our vows. The old power of words. Till death do us part.

Below that, the ad copy says, "Police are currently looking for this man for questioning in connection with several recent deaths. He is forty years old, five feet ten inches tall, weighs one hundred and eighty pounds, and has brown hair and green eyes. He's unarmed, but should be considered highly dangerous."

The man in the photo is so young and innocent. He's not me. The woman is dead. Both of these people, ghosts.

Below the photo, it says, "He now goes by the alias 'Carl Streator.' He often wears a blue tie."

Below that, it says, "If you know his whereabouts, please call 911 and ask for the police." If Oyster ran this ad or the police did, I don't know.

Helen and me standing here, looking down at the picture, Helen says, "Your wife was very pretty."

And I say, yeah, she was.

Helen's fingers, her yellow suit, her carved and varnished antique desk, they're all stained and smudged red and purple with iodine and cabbage juice. The stains smell of ammonia and vinegar. She holds the fluoroscope over the book and reads the ancient peter tracks.

"I've got a flying spell here," she says. "And one of these might be a love spell." She flips back and forth, each page smelling like cabbage farts or ammonia piss. "The culling spell," she says, "it's this one here. Ancient Zulu."

In the outer office, Mona's talking on the phone.

Helen puts her hand on my arm and pushes me back, a step

away from her desk, she says, "Watch this," and stands there, both hands pressed to her temples, her eyes closed.

I ask, what's supposed to happen?

Mona hangs up her telephone in the outer office.

The grimoire open on Helen's desk, it shifts. One corner lifts, then the opposite corner. It starts to close by itself, then opens, closes and opens, faster and faster until it rises off the desk. Her eyes still closed, Helen's lips move around silent words. Rocking and flapping, the book's a shining dark starling, hovering near the ceiling.

And the police scanner crackles and says, "Unit seventeen." It says, "Please proceed to 5680 Weeden Avenue, Northeast, the Helen Boyle real estate office, and apprehend an adult male for questioning . . ."

The grimoire hits the desk with a crash. Iodine, ammonia, vinegar, and cabbage juice splashing everywhere. Papers and books sliding to the floor.

Helen yells, "Mona!"

And I say, don't kill her, please. Don't kill her.

And Helen grabs my hand in her stained hand and says, "I think you'd better get out of here." She says, "Do you remember where we first met?" Whispering, she says, "Meet me there tonight."

In my apartment, all the tape in my answering machine is used up. In my mailbox, the bills are packed so tight I have to dig them out with a butter knife.

On the kitchen table is a shopping mall, half built. Even without the picture on the box, you can tell what it is because the parking lots are laid out. The walls are in place. The windows and doors sit off to one side, the glass installed already. The roof panels and big heating-cooling units are still in the box. The landscaping is sealed in a plastic bag.

Coming through the apartment walls, there's nothing. No one.

After weeks on the road with Helen and Mona, I've forgotten how silence was so golden.

I turn on the television. It's some black-and-white comedy about a man come back from the dead as a mule. He's supposed to teach somebody something. To save his own soul. A man's spirit occupying a mule's body.

My pager goes off again, the police, my saviors, needling me toward salvation.

The police or the manager, this place has got to be under some kind of surveillance.

On the floor, scattered all over the floors, there's the stomped fragments of a lumber mill. There's the busted ruins of a train station flecked with dried blood. Around that, a medical-dental office building lies in a billion pieces. And an airplane hangar, crushed. A ferryboat terminal, kicked apart. All the bloody ruins and artifacts of what I worked so hard to put together, all of them scattered and crackling under my shoes. What's left of my normal life.

I turn on the clock radio next to the bed. Sitting cross-legged on the floor, I reach out and scrape together the remains of gas stations and mortuaries and hamburger stands and Spanish monasteries. I pile up the bits covered with blood and dust, and the radio plays big band swing music. The radio plays Celtic folk music and ghetto rap and Indian sitar music. Piled in front of me are the parts for sanatoriums and movie studios, grain elevators and oil refineries. On the radio is electronic trance music, reggae, and waltz music. Heaped together are the parts of cathedrals and prisons and army barracks.

With the little brush and glue, I put together smokestacks and skylights and geodesic domes and minarets. Romanesque aqueducts run into Art Deco penthouses run into opium dens run into Wild West saloons run into roller coasters run into small-town Carnegie libraries run into tract houses run into college lecture halls.

After weeks on the road with Helen and Mona, I've forgotten how perfection was so important.

On my computer, there's a draft of the crib death story. The last chapter. It's the type of story that every parent and grandparent is too afraid to read and too afraid not to read. There's really no new information. The idea was to show how people cope. People move forward with their lives. We could show the deep inner well of strength and compassion each of these people discovers. That angle.

All we know about infant sudden death is there is no pattern. A baby can die in its mother's arms.

The story's still unfinished.

The best way to waste your life is by taking notes. The easiest way to avoid living is to just watch. Look for the details. Report. Don't participate. Let Big Brother do the singing and dancing for you. Be a reporter. Be a good witness. A grateful member of the audience.

On the radio, waltz music runs into punk runs into rock runs into rap runs into Gregorian chanting runs into chamber music. On television, someone is showing how to poach a salmon. Someone is showing why the *Bismarck* sank.

I glue together bay windows and groin vaults and barrel vaults and jack arches and stairways and clerestory windows and mosaic floors and steel curtain walls and half-timbered gables and Ionic pilasters.

On the radio is African drum music and French torch songs, all mixed together. On the floor in front of me are Chinese pagodas and Mexican haciendas and Cape Cod colonial houses, all combined. On television, a golfer putts. A woman wins ten thousand dollars for knowing the first line of the Gettysburg Address.

My first house I ever put together was four stories with a mansard roof and two staircases, a front one for family and a rear servant's staircase. It had metal and glass chandeliers you wired with tiny lightbulbs. It had a parquet floor in the dining room that took six weeks of cutting and gluing to piece together. It had a ceiling in the music room that my wife, Gina, stayed up late, night after night, painting with clouds and angels. It had a fireplace in the dining room with a fire I made out of cut glass with a flickering light behind it. We set the table with tiny dinner plates, and Gina stayed up at night, painting roses around the border of each plate. The two of us, those nights, with no television or radio, Katrin asleep, it seemed so important at the time. Those were the two people in that wedding photo. The house was for Katrin's second birthday. Everything had to be perfect. To be something that would prove our talent and intelligence. A masterpiece to outlive us.

Oranges and gasoline, the glue smell, mixes with the smell of shit. On my fingers, on the glue slopped there, my hands are crusted with picture windows and porches and air conditioners. Stuck to my shirt are turnstiles and escalators and trees, and I turn the radio up.

All that work and love and effort and time, my life, wasted. Everything I hoped would outlive me I've ruined.

That afternoon I came home from work and found them, I left the food in the fridge. I left the clothes in the closets. The afternoon I came home and knew what I'd done, that was the first house I stomped. An heirloom without an heir. The tiny chandeliers and glass fire and dinner plates. Stuck in my shoes, I left a trail of tiny doors and shelves and chairs and windows and blood all the way to the airport.

Beyond that, my trail ended.

And sitting here, I've run out of parts. All the walls and roofs and handrails. And what's glued to the floor in front of me is a bloody mess. It's nothing perfect or complete, but this is what I've made of my life. Right or wrong, it follows no great master plan.

All you can do is hope for a pattern to emerge, and sometimes it never does.

Still, with a plan, you only get the best you can imagine. I'd always hoped for something better than that.

A blast of French horns comes on the radio, the clatter of a Teletype, and a man's voice says how police have found yet another dead fashion model. The television shows her smiling picture. They've arrested another suspect boyfriend. Another autopsy shows signs of postmortem sexual intercourse.

My pager goes off again. The number on my page is my new savior.

My hands lumpy with shutters and doors, I pick up the phone. My fingers rough with plumbing and gutters, I dial a number I can't forget.

A man answers.

And I say, Dad. I say, Dad, it's me.

I tell him where I'm living. I tell him the name I use now. I tell him where I work. I tell him that I know how it looks, with Gina and Katrin dead, but I didn't do it. I just ran.

He says, he knows. He saw the wedding picture in today's newspaper. He knows who I am now.

A couple weeks ago, I drove by their house. I say how I saw him and Mom working in the yard. I was parked down the street, under a flowering cherry tree. My car, Helen's car, covered in pink petals. Both he and Mom, I say, they both look good.

I tell him, I've missed him, too. I love him, too. I tell him, I'm okay.

I say, I don't know what to do. I say, but it's all going to be okay.

After that, I just listen. I wait for him to stop crying so I can say I'm sorry.

Chapter 37

The Gartoller Estate in the moonlight, an eight-bedroom Georgian-style house with seven bathrooms, four fireplaces, all of it's empty and white. All of it's echoing with each step across the polished floors. The house is dark without lights. It's cold without furniture or rugs.

"Here," Helen says. "We can do it here, where no one will see us." She flicks a light switch inside a doorway.

The ceiling goes up so high it could be the sky. Light from a looming chandelier, the size of a crystal weather balloon, the light turns the tall windows into mirrors. The light throws our shadows out behind us on the wood floor. This is the fifteen-hundred-square-foot ballroom.

Me, I'm out of a job. The police are after me. My apartment stinks. My picture's full-page in the paper. I spent my day hiding in the shrubs around the front door, waiting for dark. For Helen Hoover Boyle to tell me what she has in mind.

She has the grimoire under one arm. The pages stained pink and purple. She opens it in her hands, and shows me a spell, the English words written in black pen below the foreign gibberish of the original.

"Say it," she says.

The spell?

"Read it out loud," she says.

And I ask, what's this do?

And Helen says, "Just watch out for the chandelier."

She starts reading, the words dull and even, as if she were counting, as if they were numbers. She starts reading, and her purse starts to float up from where it hangs near her waist. Her purse floats higher until it's tethered to her by the shoulder strap, floating above her head as if it were a yellow balloon.

Helen keeps reading, and my tie floats out in front of me. Rising like a blue snake out of a basket, it brushes my nose. Helen's skirt, the hem starts to rise, and she grabs it and holds it down, between her legs with one hand. She keeps reading, and my shoelaces dance in the air. Her dangle earrings, pearls and emeralds, float up alongside her ears. Her pearl necklace, it floats up around her face. It floats over her head, a hovering pearl halo.

Helen looks up at me and keeps reading.

My sport coat floats up under my arms. Helen's getting taller. She's eye level with me. Then I'm looking up at her. Her feet hang, toes pointed down, they're hanging above the floor. One yellow shoe then the other drops off and clatters on the wood.

Her voice still flat and even, Helen looks down at me and smiles.

And then one of my feet isn't touching the ground. My other foot goes limp, and I kick the way you do in deep water, trying to find the bottom of the swimming pool. I throw my hands out for purchase. I kick, and my feet pitch up behind me until I'm looking facedown at the ballroom floor four, six, eight feet below me. Me and my shadow getting farther and farther apart. My shadow getting smaller and smaller.

Helen says, "Carl, watch out."

And something cold and brittle wraps around me. Sharp bits of something loose drape around my neck and snag in my hair.

"It's the chandelier, Carl," Helen says. "Be careful."

My ass buried in the middle of the crystal beads and shards, I'm wrapped in a shivering, tinkling octopus. The cold glass arms and fake candles. My arms and legs tangle in the hanging strands of crystal chains. The dusty crystal bobs. The cobwebs and dead spiders. A hot lightbulb burns through my sleeve. This high above the floor, I panic and grab hold of a swooping glass arm, and the whole sparkling mess rocks and shakes, ringing wind chimes. Flashing bits clatter on the floor below. All of it with me inside pitches back and forth.

And Helen says, "Stop. You're going to ruin it."

Then she's next to me, floating just behind a shimmering beaded curtain of crystal. Her lips move with quiet words. Helen's pink fingernails part the beads, and she smiles in at me, saying, "Let's get you right side up, first."

The book's gone, and she holds the crystals to one side and swims closer.

I'm gripping a glass chandelier arm in both hands. The million flickering bits of it shake with my every heartbeat.

"Pretend you're underwater," she says, and unties my shoe. She slips the shoe off my foot and drops it. With her stained hands, she unties my other shoe, and the first shoe clatters on the floor. "Here," she says, and slips her arms under mine. "Take off your jacket."

She drops my jacket out of the chandelier. Then my tie. She slips out of her own jacket and lets it fall. Around us, the chandelier is a shimmering million rainbows of lead crystal. Warm with a hundred tiny lightbulbs. The burning smell of dust on all those hot lightbulbs. All of it dazzling and shivering, we're floating here in the hollow center.

We're floating in nothing but light and heat.

Helen mouths her silent words, and my heart feels full of warm water.

Helen's earrings, all her jewelry is blazing bright. All you can hear is the tinkling chimes around us. We sway less and less, and I start to let go. A million tinkling bright stars around us, this is how it must feel to be God.

And this, too, is my life.

I say, I need a place to stay. From the police. I don't know what to do next.

Holding out her hand, Helen says, "Here."

And I take it. And she doesn't let go. And we kiss. And it's nice.

And Helen says, "For now, you can stay here." She flicks a pink fingernail against a gleaming glass ball, cut and faceted to throw light in a thousand directions. She says, "From now on, we can do anything." She says, "Anything."

We kiss, and her toes peel off my socks. We kiss, and I open the buttons down the back of her blouse. My socks, her blouse, my shirt, her panty hose. Some things drop to the floor far below, some things snag and hang from the bottom of the chandelier.

My swollen infected foot, Helen's crusted, scabby knees from Oyster's attack, there's no way to hide these from each other.

It's been twenty years, but here I am, somewhere I never dreamed I'd ever be again, and I say, I'm falling in love.

And Helen, blazing smooth and hot in this center of light, she smiles and rolls her head back, saying, "That's the idea."

I'm in love with her. In love. With Helen Hoover Boyle.

My pants and her skirt flutter down into the heap, the fallen crystals, our shoes, all on the floor with the grimoire.

Chapter 38

At the offices of Helen Boyle Realty, the doors are locked, and when I knock, Mona shouts through the glass, "We're not open."

And I shout, I'm not a customer.

Inside, she's sitting at her computer, keyboarding something. Every couple keystrokes, Mona looks back and forth between the keys and the screen. On the screen, at the top in big letters, it says, "Resume."

The police scanner says a code nine-twelve.

Still keyboarding, Mona says, "I don't know why I shouldn't charge you with assault."

Maybe because she cares about me and Helen, I say.

And Mona says, "No, that's not it."

Maybe she won't blow the whistle because she still wants the grimoire.

And Mona doesn't say anything. She turns in her chair and pulls up the side of her peasant blouse. The skin on her ribs, under her arms, is white with purple blotches.

Tough love.

Through the door into Helen's office, Helen yells, "What's another word for 'tormented'?" Her desk is covered with open books. Under her desk, she's wearing one pink shoe and one yellow shoe.

The pink silk sofa, Mona's carved Louis XIV desk, the lion-legged sofa table, it's all frosted with dust. The flower arrangements are withered and brown, standing in black, stinking water.

The police scanner says a code three-eleven.

I say, I'm sorry. Grabbing her wasn't right. I pinch the crease in my pant legs and pull them up to show her the purple bruises on my shins.

"That's different," Mona says. "I was defending myself."

I stamp my foot a couple times and say my infection's a lot better. I say, thank you.

And Helen yells, "Mona? What's another way of saying 'butchered'?"

Mona says, "On your way out, we need to have a little talk."

In the inner office, Helen's facedown in an open book. It's a Hebrew dictionary. Next to it is a guide to classical Latin. Under that is a book about Aramaic. Next to that is an unfolded copy of the culling spell. The trash can next to the desk is filled with paper coffee cups.

I say, hey.

And Helen looks up. There's a coffee stain on her green lapel. The grimoire is open next to the Hebrew dictionary. And Helen blinks once, twice, three times and says, "Mr. Streator."

I ask if she'd like to get some lunch. I still need to go up against John Nash, to confront him. I was hoping she might give me something for an edge. An invisibility spell, maybe. Or a mind-control spell. Maybe something so I won't have to kill him. I come around to see what she's translating.

And Helen slides a sheet of paper on top of the grimoire, saying, "I'm a little occupied today." With a pen in one hand, she waits. With the other hand, she shuts the dictionary. She says, "Shouldn't you be hiding from the police?"

And I say, how about a movie?

And she says, "Not this weekend."

I say, how about I get us tickets to the symphony?

And Helen waves a hand between us and says, "Do what you want."

And I say, great. Then it's a date.

Helen puts her pen in the pink hair behind her ear. She opens another book and lays it on top of the Hebrew book. With one finger holding her place in a dictionary, Helen looks up and says, "It's not that I don't like you. It's just that I'm very, very busy right now."

In the open grimoire, sticking out from one edge of it is a name. Written in the margin of a page is today's name, today's assassination target. It says, Carl Streator.

Helen closes the grimoire and says, "You understand."

The police scanner says a code seven-two.

I ask if she's coming to see me, tonight, in the Gartoller house. Standing in the doorway to her office, I say I can't wait to be with her again. I need her.

And Helen smiles and says, "That's the idea."

In the outer office, Mona catches me around the wrist. She picks up her purse and loops the strap over her shoulder, yelling, "Helen, I'm going out for lunch." To me, she says, "We need to talk, but outside." She unlocks the door to let us out.

In the parking lot, standing next to my car, Mona shakes her head, saying, "You have no idea what's happening, do you?"

I'm in love. So kill me.

"With Helen?" she says. She snaps her fingers in my face and says, "You're not in love." She sighs and says, "You ever hear of a love spell?"

For whatever reason, Nash screwing dead women comes to mind.

"Helen's found a spell to trap you," Mona says. "You're in her power. You don't really love her."

I don't?

Mona stares into my eyes and says, "When was the last time you thought about burning the grimoire?" She points at the ground and says, "This? What you call love? It's just her way of dominating you."

A car drives up and parks, and inside is Oyster. He just shakes the hair back off his eyes, and sits behind the steering wheel, watching us. The shattered blond hair exploded in every direction. Two deep parallel lines, slash scars, run across each cheek. Dark red war paint.

His cell phone rings, and Oyster answers it, "Doland, Dimms and Dorn, Attorneys-at-Law."

The big power grab.

But I love Helen.

"No," Mona says. She glances at Oyster. "You just think you do. She's tricked you."

But it's love.

"I've known Helen a lot longer than you have," Mona says. She folds her arms and looks at her wristwatch. "It's not love. It's a beautiful, sweet spell, but she's making you into her slave."

Chapter 39

Experts in ancient Greek culture say that people back then didn't see their thoughts as belonging to them. When they had a thought, it occurred to them as a god or goddess giving them an order. Apollo was telling them to be brave.

Athena was telling them to fall in love.

Now people hear a commercial for sour cream potato chips and rush out to buy.

Between television and radio and Helen Hoover Boyle's magic spells, I don't know what I really want anymore. If I even believe myself, I don't know.

That night, Helen drives us to the antique store, the big warehouse where she's mutilated so much furniture. It's dark and closed, but she presses her hand over a lock and says a quick poem, and the door swings open. No burglar alarms sound. Nothing.

We're wandering deep into the maze of furniture, the dark disconnected chandeliers hanging above us. Moonlight glows in through the skylights.

"See how easy," Helen says. "We can do *anything.*"

No, I say, *she* can do anything.

Helen says, "You still love me?"

If she wants me to. I don't know. If she says so.

Helen looks up at the looming chandeliers, the hanging cages of gilt and crystal, and she says, "Got time for a quickie?"

And I say, it's not like I have a choice.

I don't know the difference between what I want and what I'm trained to want.

I can't tell what I really want and what I've been tricked into wanting.

What I'm talking about is free will. Do we have it, or does God dictate and script everything we do and say and want? Do we have free will, or do the mass media and our culture control us, our desires and actions, from the moment we're born? Do I have it, or is my mind under the control of Helen's spell?

Standing in front of a Regency armoire of burled walnut with a huge mirror of beveled glass in the door, Helen strokes the carved scrolls and garlands and says, "Become immortal with me."

Like this furniture, traveling through life after life, watching everyone who loves us die. Parasites. These armoires. Helen and I, the cockroaches of our culture.

Scarred across the mirrored door is an old gouged slash from her diamond ring. From back when she hated this immortal junk.

Imagine immortality, where even a marriage of fifty years would feel like a one-night stand. Imagine seeing trends and fashions blur past you. Imagine the world more crowded and desperate every century. Imagine changing religions, homes, diets, careers, until none of them have any real value. Imagine traveling the world until you're bored with every square inch. Imagine your emotions, your loves and hates and rivalries and victories, played out again and again until life is nothing more than a melo-dramatic soap opera. Until you regard the birth and death of other people with no more emotion than the wilted cut flowers you throw away.

I tell Helen, I think we're immortal already.

She says, "I have the power." She snaps open her purse and fishes out a sheet of folded paper, she shakes the paper open and says, "Do you know about 'scrying'?"

I don't know what I know. I don't know what's true. I doubt I really know anything. I say, tell me.

Helen slips a silk scarf from around her neck and wipes the dust off the huge mirrored door of the armoire. The Regency armoire with inlaid olive-wood carvings and Second Empire fire-gilded hardware, according to the index card taped to it. She says, "Witches spread oil on a mirror, then they say a spell, and they can read the future in the mirror."

The future, I say, great. Cheatgrass. Kudzu. The Nile perch.

Right now, I'm not even sure I can read the present.

Helen holds up the paper and reads. In the dull, counting voice she used for the flying spell, she reads a few quick lines. She lowers the paper and says, "Mirror, mirror, tell us what our future will be if we love each other and use our new power."

Her new power.

"I made up the 'mirror, mirror' part," Helen says. She slips her hand around mine and squeezes, but I don't squeeze back. She says, "I tried this at the office with the mirror in my compact, and it was like watching television through a microscope."

In the mirror, our reflections blur, the shapes swim together, the reflection mixes into an even gray.

"Tell us," Helen says, "show us our future together."

And shapes appear in the gray. Light and shadows swim together.

"See," she says. "There we are. We're young again. I can do that. You look like you did in the newspaper. The wedding photo."

Everything's so unfocused. I don't know what I see.

"And look," Helen says. She tosses her chin toward the mirror. "We're ruling the world. We're founding a dynasty."

But *what's enough?* I can hear Oyster say, him and his overpopulation talk.

Power, money, food, sex, love. Can we ever get enough, or will getting some make us crave even more?

Inside the shifting mess of the future, I can't recognize anything. I can't see anything except just more of the past. More problems, more people. Less biodiversity. More suffering.

"I see us together forever," she says.

I say, if that's what she wants.

And Helen says, "What's that supposed to mean?"

Just whatever she wants it to mean, I say. She's the one pulling the strings here. She's the one planting her little seeds. Colonizing me. Occupying me. The mass media, the culture, everything laying its eggs under my skin. Big Brother filling me with need.

Do I really want a big house, a fast car, a thousand beautiful sex partners? Do I really want these things? Or am I trained to want them?

Are these things really better than the things I already have? Or am I just trained to be dissatisfied with what I have now? Am I just under a spell that says nothing is ever good enough?

The gray in the mirror is mixing, swirling, it could be anything. No matter what the future holds, ultimately it will be a disappointment.

And Helen takes my other hand. Holding both my hands in hers, she pulls me around, saying, "Look at me." She says, "Did Mona say something to you?"

I say, you love you. I just don't want to be used anymore.

Above us are the chandeliers, glowing silver in the moonlight.

"What did Mona say?" Helen says.

And I'm counting 1, counting 2, counting 3 . . .

"Don't do this," Helen says. "I love you." Squeezing my hands, she says, "Do not shut me out."

I'm counting 4, counting 5, counting 6 . . .

"You're being just like my husband," she says. "I just want you to be happy."

That's easy, I say, just put a "happy" spell on me.

And Helen says, "There's no such spell." She says, "They have drugs for that."

I don't want to keep making the world worse. I want to try and clean up this mess we've made. The population. The environment. The culling spell. The same magic that ruins my life is supposed to fix it.

"But we can do that," Helen says. "With more spells."

Spells to fix spells to fix spells to fix spells, and life just gets more miserable in ways we never imagined. That's the future I see in the mirror.

Mr. Eugene Schieffelin and his starlings, Spencer Baird and his carp, history is filled with brilliant people who wanted to fix things and just made them worse.

I want to burn the grimoire.

I tell her about what Mona told me. About how she's put a spell on me to make me her immortal love slave for all of eternity.

"Mona's lying," Helen says.

But how do I know that? Whom do I believe?

The gray in the mirror, the future, maybe it's not clear to me because now nothing's clear to me.

And Helen drops my hands. She waves her hands at the Regency armoires, the Federalist desks and Italian Renaissance coat racks, and says, "So if reality is all a spell, and you don't really want what you think you want . . ." She pushes her face in my face and says, "If you have no free will. You don't really *know* what you *know*. You don't really *love* who you *only think* you love. What do you have left to live for?"

Nothing.

This is just us standing here with all the furniture watching.

Think of deep outer space, the incredible cold and quiet where your wife and kid wait.

And I say, please. I tell her to give me her cell phone.

The gray still shifting and liquid in the mirror, Helen snaps open her purse and hands me the phone.

I flip it open and dial 911.

And a woman's voice says, "Police, fire, or medical?"

And I say, medical.

"Your location?" the voice says.

And I tell her the address of the bar on Third where Nash and I meet, the bar near the hospital.

"And the nature of your medical emergency?"

Forty professional cheerleaders overcome with heat exhaustion. A women's volleyball team needing mouth-to-mouth. A crew of fashion models wanting breast examinations. I tell her, if they've got an emergency med tech named John Nash, he's the one to send. I tell her, if they can't find Nash, not to bother.

Helen takes the phone back. She looks at me, blinking once, twice, three times, slow, and says, "What are you up to?"

What I have left, maybe the only way to find freedom, is by doing the things I don't want to. Stop Nash. Confess to the police. Accept my punishment.

I need to rebel against myself.

It's the opposite of following your bliss. I need to do what I most fear.

Chapter 40

Nash is eating a bowl of chili. He's at a back table in the bar on Third Avenue. The bartender is slumped forward on the bar, his arms still swinging above the barstools. Two men and two women are facedown at a booth table. Their cigarettes still burn in an ashtray, only half burned down. Another man is laid out in the doorway to the bathrooms. Another man is dead, stretched out on the pool table, the cue still clutched in his hands. Behind the bar, there's a radio blaring static in the kitchen. Somebody in a greasy apron is facedown on the grill among the hamburgers, the grill popping and smoking and the sweet, greasy smoke from the guy's face rolling out along the ceiling.

The candle on Nash's table is the only light in the place.

And Nash looks up, chili red around his mouth, and says, "I thought you'd like a little privacy for this."

He's wearing his white uniform. A dead body nearby is wearing the same uniform. "My partner," Nash says, nodding at the body. As he nods, his ponytail, the little black palm tree, flops around on top of his head. Red chili stains run down the front of his uniform. Nash says, "Me culling him was long overdue."

Behind me, the street door opens and a man steps in. He stands there, looking around. He waves a hand through the smoke and looks around, saying, "What the fuck?" The street door shuts behind him.

And Nash tucks his chin and fishes two fingers inside his chest pocket. He brings out a white index card smeared with red and yellow food and he reads the culling song, his words flat and steady as someone counting out loud. As Helen.

The man in the doorway, his eyes roll up white. His knees buckle and he slumps to one side.

I just stand here.

Nash tucks the index card back in his pocket and says, "Now, where were we?"

So, I say, where did he find the poem?

And Nash says, "Guess." He says, "I got it the only place where you can't destroy it."

He picks up a bottle of beer and points the long neck at me, saying, "Think." He says, "Think hard."

The book, *Poems and Rhymes from Around the World*, will always be out there for people to find. Hiding in plain sight. Just in this one place, he says. No way can it ever be rooted out.

For whatever reason, cheatgrass comes to mind. And zebra mussels. And Oyster.

Nash drinks some beer and sets it down and says, "Think hard."

I say, the fashion models, the killings. I say, what he's doing is wrong.

And Nash says, "You give up?"

He has to see that having sex with dead women is wrong.

Nash picks up his spoon and says, "The good old Library of Congress. Your tax dollars at work."

Damn.

He digs the spoon into the bowl of chili. He puts the spoon in his mouth and says, "And don't lecture me about the evils of necrophilia." He says, "You're about the last person who can give that lecture." His mouth full of chili, Nash says, "I know who you are."

He swallows and says, "You're still wanted for questioning."

He licks the chili smeared around his lips and says, "I saw your wife's death certificate." He smiles and says, "Signs of post-mortem sexual intercourse?"

Nash points at an empty chair, and I sit.

"Don't tell me," he leans across the table and says. "Don't tell me it wasn't just about the best sex you've ever had."

And I say, shut up.

"You can't kill me," Nash says. He crumbles a handful of crackers into his bowl and says, "You and me, we're exactly alike."

And I say, it was different. She was my wife.

"Your wife or not," Nash says, "dead means dead. It's still necrophilia."

Nash jabs his spoon around in the crackers and red and says, "You killing me would be the same as you killing yourself."

I say, shut up.

"Relax," he says. "I didn't give nobody a letter about this." Nash crunches a mouthful of crackers and red. "That would've been stupid," he says. "I mean, think." And he shovels in more chili. "All's they'd have to do is read it, and I don't need the competition."

Imperfect and messy, this is the world I live in. This far from God, these are the people I'm left with. Everybody grabbing for power. Mona and Helen and Nash and Oyster. The only people who know me hate me. We all hate each other. We all fear each other. The whole world is my enemy.

"You and me," Nash says, "we can't trust nobody."

Welcome to hell.

If Mona is right, Karl Marx's words coming out of her mouth, then killing Nash would be saving him. Returning him to God. Connecting him to humanity by resolving his sins.

My eyes meet his eyes, and Nash's lips start to move. His breath is nothing but chili.

He's saying the culling song. As hard as a dog barking, he says each word so hard that chili bubbles out around his mouth. Drops of red fly out. He stops and looks into his chest pocket. His hand digs to find his index card. With two fingers, he holds it and starts to read. The card is so smeared he rubs it on the tablecloth and starts to read again.

It sounds heavy and rich. It's the sound of doom.

My eyes relax and the world blurs into unfocused gray. All my muscles go smooth and long. My eyes roll up and my knees start to fold.

This is how it feels to die. To be saved.

But by now, killing is a reflex. It's the way I solve everything.

My knees fold, and I hit the floor in three stages, my ass, my back, my head.

As fast as a belch, a sneeze, a yawn from deep inside me, the culling song whips through my mind. The powder keg of all my unresolved shit, it never fails me.

The gray comes back into focus. Flat on my back on the bar floor, I see the greasy, gray smoke roll along the ceiling. You can hear the guy's face still frying.

Nash, his two fingers let the card drop onto the table. His eyes roll up. His shoulders heave, and his face lands in the bowl of chili. Red flies everywhere. The bulk of his body in his white uniform, it heaves over and Nash hits the floor next to me. His eyes look into my eyes. His face smeared with chili. His ponytail, the little black palm tree on the top of his head, it's come loose and the stringy black hair hangs limp across his cheeks and forehead.

He's saved, but I'm not.

The greasy smoke settling over me, the grill popping and sizzling, I pick up Nash's index card off the floor. I hold it over the candle on the table, adding smoke to the smoke, and I just watch it burn.

A siren goes off, the smoke alarm, so loud I can't hear myself think. As if I ever think. As if I ever could think. The siren fills me. Big Brother. It occupies my mind, the way an army does a city. While I sit and wait for the police to save me. To deliver me to God and reunite me with humanity, the siren wails, drowning out everything. And I'm glad.

Chapter 41

This is after the police read me my rights. After they cuff my hands behind my back and drive me to the precinct. This is after the first patrolman arrived at the scene, looked at the dead bodies, and said, "Sweet, suffering Christ." After the paramedics rolled the dead cook off the grill, took one look at his fried face, and puked in their own cupped hands. This is after the police gave me my one phone call, and I called Helen and said I was sorry, but this was it. I was arrested. And Helen said, "Don't worry. I'll save you." After they fingerprinted me and took a mug shot. After they confiscated my wallet and keys and watch. They put my clothes, my brown sport coat and blue tie, in a plastic bag tagged with my new criminal number. After the police walked me down a cold, cinder-block hallway, naked into a cold concrete room. After they leave me alone with a beefy, buzz-cut old officer with hands the size of a catcher's mitt. Alone in a room with nothing but a desk, my bag of clothes, and a jar of petroleum jelly.

After I'm alone with this grizzled old ox, he pulls on a latex glove and says, "Please turn to the wall, bend over, and use your hands to spread your ass cheeks."

And I say, what?

And this big frowning giant wipes two gloved fingers around in the jar of petroleum jelly and says, "Body cavity search." He says, "Now turn around."

And I'm counting 1, counting 2, counting 3 . . .

And I turn around. I bend over. One hand gripping each half of my ass, I pull them apart.

Counting 4, counting 5, counting 6 . . .

Me and my failed Ethics. The same as Waltraud Wagner and Jeffrey Dahmer and Ted Bundy, I'm a serial killer and this is how my punishment starts. Proof of my free will. This is my path to salvation.

And the cop's voice, all rough with the smell of cigarettes, he says, "Standard procedure for all detainees considered dangerous."

I'm counting 7, counting 8, counting 9 . . .

And the cop growls, "You're going to feel a slight pressure so just relax."

And I'm counting 10, counting 11, counting . . .

And damn.

Damn!

"Relax," the cop says.

Damn. Damn. Damn. Damn. Damn. Damn!

The pain, it's worse than Mona poking me with her red-hot tweezers. It's worse than the rubbing alcohol washing away my blood. I grip the two handfuls of my ass and grit my teeth, the sweat running down my legs. Sweat from my forehead drips off my nose. My breathing stops. The drips fall straight down and splash between my bare feet, my feet planted wide apart.

Something huge and hard twists deeper into me, and the cop's horrible voice says, "Yeah, relax, buddy."

And I'm counting 12, counting 13...

The twisting stops. The huge, hard thing backs off, slow, almost all the way. Then it twists in deep again. Slow as the hour hand on a clock, then faster, the cop's greased fingers prod into me, retreat, prod in, retreat.

And close to my ear, the cop's gravel and ashtray old voice says, "Hey, buddy, you got time for a quickie?"

And my whole body does a spasm.

And the cop says, "Boy howdy, somebody just got tight."

I say, Officer. Please. You have no idea. I could kill you. Please don't do this.

And the cop says, "Let go of me so I can unlock your handcuffs. It's me, Helen."

Helen?

"Helen Hoover Boyle? Remember?" the cop says. "Two nights ago, you were doing almost this exact same thing to me inside a chandelier?"

Helen?

The huge hard something still twisted deep inside me.

The cop says, "This is called an *occupation spell*. I translated it just a couple hours ago. I've got Officer whoever here crammed down into his subconscious right now. I'm running his show."

The hard cold sole of the officer's shoe shoves against my ass, and the huge hard fingers yank themselves out. Between my feet is a puddle of sweat. Still gritting my teeth, I stand up, fast.

The officer looks at his fingers and says, "I thought I was going to lose these." He smells the fingers and makes a nasty face.

Great, I say, breathing deep, eyes closed. First she's controlling me, now I have to worry about Helen controlling everyone around me.

And the cop says, "I had control of Mona for the last couple of hours this afternoon. Just to give the spell a test run, and to get even with her for scaring you, I gave her a little makeover."

The cop grabs his crotch. "This is amazing. Being with you like this, you're giving me an erection." He says, "This sounds sexist, but I've always wanted a penis."

I say, I don't want to hear this.

And Helen says, through the cop's mouth, she says, "I think as soon as I put you into a taxi, maybe I'll hang around in this guy and beat off. Just for the experience."

And I say, if you think this will make me love you, think again.

A tear runs down the cop's cheek.

Standing here naked, I say, I don't want you. I can't trust you.

"You can't love me," the cop says, Helen says in the cop's grizzled voice, "because I'm a woman and I have more power than you."

And I say, just go, Helen. Get the fuck out of here. I don't need you. I want to pay for my crimes. I'm tired of making the world wrong to justify my own bad behavior.

And the cop's crying hard now, and another cop walks in. It's a young cop, and he looks from the old cop, crying, to me, naked. The young cop says, "Everything A-okay in here, Sarge?"

"It's just delightful," the old cop says, wiping his eyes. "We're having a wonderful time." He sees he's wiped his eyes with his gloved hand, the fingers out my ass, and he tears off the glove with a little scream. His whole body does a big shudder, and he throws the greasy glove across the room.

I tell the young cop, we were just having a little talk.

And the young cop puts a fist in my face and says, "You just shut the fuck up."

The old cop, Sarge, sits down on the edge of the desk and crosses his legs at the knee. He sniffs back tears and tosses his head as if tossing back hair and says, "Now, if you don't mind, we'd very much like to be alone."

I just look at the ceiling.

The young cop says, "Sure thing, Sarge."

And Sarge grabs a tissue and dabs his eyes.

Then the young cop turns fast, grabbing me under the jaw and jamming me up against the wall. My back and legs against the cold concrete. With my head pushed up and back, the young cop's hand squeezing my throat, the cop says, "You don't give the Sarge a hard time!" He shouts, "Got that?"

And the Sarge looks up with a weak smile and says, "Yeah. You heard him." And sniffs.

And the young cop lets loose of my throat. He steps back toward the door, saying, "I'll be out front if you need . . . well, anything."

"Thank you," the Sarge says. He clutches the young cop's hand, squeezing it, saying, "You're too sweet."

And the young cop jerks his hand away and leaves the room.

Helen's inside this man, the way a television plants its seed in you. The way cheatgrass takes over a landscape. The way a song stays in your head. The way ghosts haunt houses. The way a germ infects you. The way Big Brother occupies your attention.

The Sarge, Helen, gets to his feet. He fiddles with his holster and pulls out his gun. Holding the pistol in both hands, he points it at me and says, "Now get your clothes out of the bag and put them on." The Sarge sniffs back tears and kicks the garbage bag full of clothes at me and says, "Get dressed, damn it." He says, "I came here to save you."

The pistol trembling, the Sarge says, "I want you out of here so I can beat off."

Chapter 42

Everywhere, words are mixing. Words and lyrics and dialogue are mixing in a soup that could trigger a chain reaction. Maybe acts of God are just the right combination of media junk thrown out into the air. The wrong words collide and call up an earthquake. The way rain dances called storms, the right combination of words might call down tornadoes. Too many advertising jingles commingling could be behind global warming. Too many television reruns bouncing around might cause hurricanes. Cancer. AIDS.

In the taxi, on my way to the Helen Boyle real estate offices, I see newspaper headlines mixing with hand-lettered signs. Leaflets stapled to telephone poles mix with third-class mail. The songs of street buskers mix with Muzak mix with street hawkers mix with talk radio.

We're living in a teetering tower of babble. A shaky reality of words. A DNA soup for disaster. The natural world destroyed, we're left with this cluttered world of language.

Big Brother is singing and dancing, and we're left to watch. Sticks and stones may break our bones, but our role is just to be a good audience. To just pay our attention and wait for the next disaster.

Against the taxi's seat, my ass still feels greasy and stretched out.

There are thirty-three copies of the poems book left to find. We need to visit the Library of Congress. We need to mop up the mess and make sure it will never happen.

We need to warn people. My life is over. This is my new life.

The taxi pulls into the parking lot, and Mona's outside the front doors, locking them with a huge ring of keys. For a minute, she could be Helen. Mona, her hair's ratted, back-combed, teased into a red and black bubble. She's wearing a brown suit, but not chocolate brown. It's more the brown of a chocolate hazelnut truffle served on a satin pillow in a luxury hotel.

A box sits on the ground at Mona's feet. On top of the box is something red, a book. The grimoire.

I'm walking across the parking lot, and she calls, "Helen's not here."

There was something on the police scanner about everybody in a bar on Third Avenue being dead, Mona says, and me being arrested. Putting the box in the trunk of her car, she says, "You just missed Mrs. Boyle. She ran out of here sobbing just a second ago."

The Sarge.

Helen's big, leather-smelling Realtor's car is nowhere in sight.

Looking down at her own brown high heels, her tailored suit, padded and tucked, doll clothes with huge topaz buttons, her short skirt, Mona says, "Don't ask me how *this* happened." She holds up her hands, her black fingernails painted pink with white tips. Mona says, "Please tell Mrs. Boyle I don't appreciate having my body kidnapped and shit done to me." She points at her own stiff bubble of hair, her blusher cheeks and pink lipstick, and says, "*This* is the equivalent of a fashion rape."

With her new pink fingernails, Mona slams the trunk lid.

Pointing at my shirt, she says, "Did things with your friend get a little bloody?"

The red stains are chili, I tell her.

The grimoire, I say. I saw it. The red human skin. The pentagram tattoo.

"She gave it to me," Mona says. She snaps open her little brown purse and reaches inside, saying, "She said she wouldn't need it anymore. Like I said, she was upset. She was crying."

With two pink fingernails, Mona plucks a folded paper out of her purse. It's a page from the grimoire, the page with my name written on it, and she holds it out to me, saying, "Take care of yourself. I guess somebody in some government must want you dead."

Mona says, "I guess Helen's little love spell must've backfired." She stumbles in her brown high heels, and leaning on the car, she says, "Believe it or not, we're doing this to save you."

Oyster's slumped in her backseat, too still, too perfect, to be alive. His shattered blond hair spreads across the seat. The Hopi medicine bag still hangs around his neck, cigarettes falling out of it. The red scars across his cheeks from Helen's car keys.

I ask, is he dead?

And Mona says, "You wish." She says, "No, he'll be okay." She gets into the driver's seat and starts the car, saying, "You'd better hurry and go find Helen. I think she might do something desperate."

She slams her car door and starts to back out of her parking space.

Through her car window, Mona yells, "Check at the New Continuum Medical Center." She drives off, yelling, "I just hope you're not too late."

Chapter 43

In room 131 at the New Continuum Medical Center, the floor sparkles. The linoleum tile snaps and pops as I walk across it, across the shards and slivers of red and green, yellow and blue. The drops of red. The diamonds and rubies, emeralds and sapphires. Both Helen's shoes, the pink and the yellow, the heels are hammered down to mush. The ruined shoes left in the middle of the room.

Helen stands on the far side of the room, in a little lamplight, just the edge of some light from a table lamp. She's leaning on a cabinet made of stainless steel. Her hands are spread against the steel. She presses her cheek there.

My shoes snap and crush the colors on the floor, and Helen turns.

There's a smear of blood across her pink lipstick. On the

cabinet is a kiss of pink and red. Where she was lying is a blurry gray window, and inside is something too perfect and white to be alive.

Patrick.

The frost around the edges of the window has started to melt, and water drips down the cabinet.

And Helen says, "You're here," and her voice is blurry and thick. Blood spills out of her mouth.

Just looking at her, my foot aches.

I'm okay, I say.

And Helen says, "I'm glad."

Her cosmetic case is dumped out on the floor. Among the shards of color are twisted chains and settings, gold and platinum. Helen says, "I tried to break the biggest ones," and she coughs into her hand. "The rest I tried to chew," she says, and coughs until her palm is filled with blood and slivers of white.

Next to the cosmetic case is a spilled bottle of liquid drain cleaner, the spill a green puddle around it.

Her teeth are shattered, bloody gaps, and pits show inside her mouth. She puts her face against the gray window. Her breath fogging the glass, her bloody hand goes to the side of her skirt.

"I don't want to go back to how it was before," she says, "the way my life was before I met you." She wipes her bloody hand and keeps wiping it on her skirt. "Even with all the power in the world."

I say, we need to get her to a hospital.

And Helen smiles a bloody smile and says, "This is a hospital."

It's nothing personal, she says. She just needed someone. Even if she could bring Patrick back, she'd never want to ruin his life by sharing the culling spell. Even if it meant living alone again, she'd never want Patrick to have that power.

"Look at him," she says, and touches the gray glass with her pink fingernails. "He's so perfect."

She swallows, blood and shattered diamonds and teeth, and

makes a terrible wrinkled face. Her hands clutch her stomach, and she leans on the steel cabinet, the gray window. Blood and condensation run down from the little window.

With one shaking hand, Helen snaps open her purse and takes out a lipstick. She touches it around her lips and the pink lipstick comes away smeared with blood.

She says she's unplugged the cryogenic unit. Disconnected the alarm and backup batteries. She wants to die with Patrick.

She wants it to end here. The culling spell. The power. The loneliness. She wants to destroy all the jewels that people think will save them. All the residue that outlasts the talent and intelligence and beauty. All the decorative junk left behind by real accomplishment and success. She wants to destroy all the lovely parasites that outlive their human hosts.

The purse drops out of her hands. On the floor, the gray rock rolls out of the purse. For whatever reason, Oyster comes to mind.

Helen belches. She takes a tissue from her purse and cups it under her mouth and spits out blood and bile and broken emeralds. Flashing inside her mouth, stuck in the shredded meat of her gums are jagged pink sapphires and shattered orange beryls. Lodged in the roof of her mouth are fragments of purple spinels. Sunk in her tongue are shards of black bort diamond.

And Helen smiles and says, "I want to be with my family." She wraps the bloody tissue into a ball and tucks it inside the cuff of her suit. Her earrings, her necklaces, her rings, it's all gone.

The details of her suit are, it's some color. It's a suit. It's ruined. She says, "Please. Just hold me."

Inside the gray window, the perfect infant is curled on its side in a pillow of white plastic. One thumb is in its mouth. Perfect and pale as blue ice.

I put my arms around Helen and she winces.

Her knees start to fold, and I lower her to the floor. Helen Hoover Boyle closes her eyes. She says, "Thank you, Mr. Streator."

With the gray rock in my fist, I punch through the cold gray window. My hands bleeding, I lift out Patrick, cold and pale. My blood on Patrick, I put him in Helen's arms. I put my arms around Helen.

My blood and hers, mixed now.

Lying in my arms, Helen closes her eyes and grinds her head into my lap. She smiles and says, "Didn't it feel too coincidental when Mona found the grimoire?"

Leering at me, she opens her eyes and says, "Wasn't it just a little too neat and tidy, the fact that we'd been traveling along with the grimoire the whole time?"

Helen lying in my arms, she cradles Patrick. Then it happens. She reaches up and pinches my cheek. Helen looks up at me and smiles with just half her mouth, a leer with blood and green bile between her lips. She winks and says, "Gotcha, Dad!"

My whole body, one muscle spasm wet with sweat.

Helen says, "Did you really think Mom would off herself over *you*? And trash her precious fucking jewels? And thaw this frozen piece of meat?" She laughs, blood and drain cleaner bubbling in her throat, and says, "Did you really think Mom would *chew* her fucking diamonds because you didn't love her?"

I say, Oyster?

"In the flesh," Helen says, Oyster says with Helen's mouth, Helen's voice. "Well, I'm in Mrs. Boyle's flesh, but I bet you've been inside her yourself."

Helen raises Patrick in her hands. Her child, cold and blue as porcelain. Frozen fragile as glass.

And she tosses the dead child across the room where it clatters against the steel cabinet and falls to the floor, spinning on the linoleum. Patrick. A frozen arm breaks off. Patrick. The spinning body hits a steel cabinet corner and the legs snap off. Patrick. The armless, legless body, a broken doll, it spins against the wall and the head breaks off.

And Helen winks and says, "Come on, Dad. Don't flatter your-self."

And I say, damn you.

Oyster occupies Helen, the way an army occupies a city. The way Helen occupied Sarge. The way the past, the media, the world, occupy you.

Helen says, Oyster says through Helen's mouth, "Mona's known about the grimoire for weeks now. The first time she saw Mom's planner, she knew." He says, "She just couldn't translate it."

Oyster says, "My thing is music, and Mona's thing is . . . well, stupidity is Mona's thing."

With Helen's voice, he says, "This afternoon, Mona woke up in some beauty salon, getting her nails painted pink." He says, "She stormed back to the office, she found Mrs. Boyle facedown on her desk in some kind of a coma."

Helen shudders and grabs her stomach. She says, "Open in front of Mrs. Boyle was a translated spell, called an occupation spell. In fact all the spells were translated."

She says, Oyster says, "God bless Mom and her crossword puz-zles. She's in here somewhere, mad as hell."

Oyster says, through Helen's mouth says, "Say hi to Mom for me."

The brittle blue statue, the frozen baby, is shattered, broken among the broken jewels, a busted-off finger here, the broken-off legs there, the shattered head.

I say, so now he and Mona are going to kill everybody and be-come Adam and Eve?

Every generation wants to be the last.

"Not everybody," Helen says. "We're going to need some slaves."

With Helen's bloody hands, he reaches down and pulls her skirt up. Grabbing her crotch, he says, "Maybe you and Mom will have time for a quickie before she's toast."

And I heave Helen's body off my lap.

My whole body aching more than my foot ever ached.

Helen cries out, a little scream as she slides to the floor. And curled there on the cold linoleum with the shattered gems and fragments of Patrick, she says, "Carl?"

She puts a hand to her mouth, feels the jewels embedded there. She twists to look at me and says, "Carl? Carl, where am I?"

She sees the stainless-steel cabinet, the broken gray window. She sees the little blue arms first. Then the legs. The head. And she says, "No."

Spraying blood, Helen says, "No! No! No!" and crawling through the sharp slivers of broken color, her voice thick and blurred from her ruined teeth, she grabs all the pieces. Sobbing, covered in bile and blood, the room stinking, she clutches the broken blue pieces. The hands and tiny feet, the crushed torso and dented head, she hugs them to her chest and screams, "Oh, Patrick! Patty!"

She screams, "Oh, my Patty-Pat-Pat! No!"

Kissing the dented blue head, squeezing it to her breast, she asks, "What's happening? Carl, help me." She stares at me until a cramp bends her in half and she sees the empty bottle of liquid drain cleaner.

"God, Carl, help me," she says, clutching her child and rocking. "God, please tell me how I got here!"

And I go to her. I take her in my arms and say, at first, the new owner pretends he never looked at the living room floor. Never really looked. Not the first time they toured the house. Not when the inspector showed them through it. They'd measured rooms and told the movers where to set the couch and piano, hauled in everything they owned, and never really stopped to look at the living room floor. They pretend.

Helen's head is nodding forward over Patrick. The blood's drooling from her mouth. Her arms are looser, spilling little fingers and toes onto the floor.

In another moment, I'll be alone. This is my life. And I swear, no matter where or when, I'll track down Oyster and Mona.

What's good is this only takes a minute.

It's an old song about animals going to sleep. It's wistful and sentimental, and my face feels livid and hot with oxygenated hemoglobin while I say the poem out loud under the fluorescent lights, with the loose bundle of Helen in my arms, leaning back against the steel cabinet. Patrick's covered in my blood, covered in her blood. Her mouth is open a little, her glittering teeth are real diamonds.

Her name was Helen Hoover Boyle. Her eyes were blue.

My job is to notice the details. To be an impartial witness. Everything is always research. My job isn't to feel anything.

It's called a culling song. In some ancient cultures, they sang it to children during famines or droughts, anytime the tribe had outgrown its land. It was sung to warriors injured in accidents or the very old or anyone dying. It was used to end misery and pain.

It's a lullaby.

I say, everything will be all right. I hold Helen, rocking her, telling her, rest now. Telling her, everything is going to be just fine.

Chapter 44

W hen I was twenty years old, I married a woman named Gina Dinji, and that was supposed to be the rest of my life. A year later, we had a daughter named Katrin, and she was supposed to be the rest of my life. Then Gina and Katrin died. And I ran and became Carl Streator. And I became a journalist. And for twenty more years, that was my life.

After that, well, you already know what happened.

How long I held on to Helen Hoover Boyle I don't know. After long enough, it was just her body. It was so long she'd stopped bleeding. By then, the broken parts of Patrick Boyle, still cradled in her arms, they'd thawed enough to start bleeding.

By then, footsteps arrived outside the door to room 131. The door opened.

Me still sitting on the floor, Helen and Patrick dead in my arms, the door opens, and it's the grizzled old Irish cop.

Sarge.

And I say, please. Please, put me in jail. I'll plead guilty to anything. I killed my wife. I killed my kid. I'm Waltraud Wagner, the Angel of Death. Kill me so I can be with Helen again.

And the Sarge says, "We need to get a move on." He steps from the doorway to the steel cabinet. On a pad of paper, he writes something in pen. He tears off the note and hands it to me.

His wrinkled hand is spotted with moles, carpeted with gray hairs. His fingernails, thick and yellow.

"Please forgive me for taking my own life," the note says. "I'm with my son now."

It's Helen's handwriting, the same as in her planner book, the grimoire.

It's signed, "Helen Hoover Boyle," in her exact handwriting.

And I look from the body in my arms, the blood and green drain-cleaner vomit, to the Sarge standing there, and I say, Helen?

"In the flesh," the Sarge says, Helen says. "Well, not my own flesh," he says, and looks at Helen's body dead in my lap. He looks at his own wrinkled hands and says, "I hate ready-to-wear, but any port in a storm."

So this is how we're on the road again.

Sometimes I worry that Sarge here is really Oyster pretending to be Helen occupying the Sarge. When I sleep with whoever this is, I pretend it's Mona. Or Gina. So it all comes out even.

According to Mona Sabbat, people who eat or drink too much, people addicted to drugs or sex or stealing, they're really controlled by spirits that loved those things too much to quit after death. Drunks and kleptos, they're possessed by evil spirits.

You are the culture medium. The host.

Some people still think they run their own lives.

You are the possessed.

We're all of us haunting and haunted.

Something foreign is always living itself through you. Your whole life is the vehicle for something to come to earth.

An evil spirit. A theory. A marketing campaign. A political strategy. A religious doctrine.

Driving me away from the New Continuum Medical Center in a squad car, the Sarge says, "They have the occupation spell and the flying spell." He ticks off each spell by holding up another finger. "They'll have a resurrection spell—but it only works on animals. Don't ask me why," he says. She says, "They have a rain spell and a sun spell... a fertility spell to make crops grow... a spell to communicate with animals..."

Not looking at me, looking at his fingers spread on the steering wheel, the Sarge says, "They do not have a love spell."

So I am really in love with Helen. A woman in a man's body. We don't have hot sex anymore, but as Nash would say, how is that different than most love relationships after long enough?

Mona and Oyster have the grimoire, but they don't have the culling song. The grimoire page that Mona gave me, the one with my name written in the margin, it's the song. Along the bottom of the page is written, "I want to save the world, too—but not Oyster's way." It's signed, "Mona."

"They don't have the culling song," the Sarge says, Helen says, "but they have a shield spell."

A shield spell?

To protect them from the culling song, the Sarge says.

"But not to worry," he says. "I have a badge and a gun and a penis."

To find Mona and Oyster, you only have to look for the fantastic, for miracles. The amazing tabloid headlines. The young couple seen crossing Lake Michigan on foot in July. The girl who made grass grow up, green and tall, through the snow for buffalo starving in Canada. The boy who talks to lost dogs at the animal shelter and helps them get home.

Look for magic. Look for saints.

The Flying Madonna. The Roadkill Jesus Christ. The Ivy Inferno. The Talking Judas Cow.

Keep going after the facts. Witch-hunting. This isn't what a therapist will tell you to do, but it works.

Mona and Oyster, this will be their world soon enough. The power has shifted. Helen and I will be forever playing catch-up. Imagine if Jesus chased you around, trying to catch you and save your soul. Not just a patient passive God, but a hardworking, aggressive bloodhound.

The Sarge snaps open his holster, the way Helen used to snap open her little purse, and he takes out a pistol.

He says, Helen says, whoever says, "How about we just kill them the old-fashioned way?"

Now this is my life.

About the Author

Chuck Palahniuk's four novels are the bestselling *Fight Club*, which was made into a film by director David Fincher, *Survivor*, *Invisible Monsters*, and *Choke*. He lives in Portland, Oregon.